SHOCKWAVE

For Leah,
who really wanted Replica 2

STERLING CHILDREN'S BOOKS
New York

An Imprint of Sterling Publishing Co., Inc.
122 Fifth Avenue
New York, NY 10011

Text © 2016 Jack Heath
Interior illustrations © 2016 Scholastic Australia
Cover © 2020 Sterling Publishing Co., Inc.

Previously published by Scholastic Australia 2016

ISBN 978-1-4549-3845-3
978-1-4549-3848-4 (e-book)

For information about custom editions, special sales, and premium
and corporate purchases, please contact Sterling Special Sales
at 800-805-5489 or specialsales@sterlingpublishing.com.

Manufactured in the United States of America

Lot #:
2 4 6 8 10 9 7 5 3 1
09/20

sterlingpublishing.com

Cover art and title page by Peter Ware
Cover design by Julie Robine

Image credits: flame border: Natutik/Shutterstock.com

JACK HEATH

SHOCKWAVE

PICK YOUR FATE

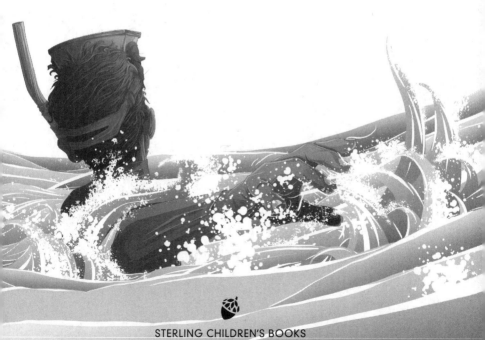

STERLING CHILDREN'S BOOKS
New York

30:00

A dark shape wobbles beneath the water, getting closer to the beach. You're ninety-nine percent sure it's just seaweed drifting on the current—but what if it isn't? What if it's one of those big saltwater crocodiles Harrison warned you about?

You look up and down the beach. There are crushed shells, dead jellyfish, and a shapeless mountain that might once have been an epic sandcastle—but no people. No one to ask for advice. Nobody who will call for help if something happens to you. You didn't even tell anyone you were going surfing, which now seems like a mistake.

Maybe you shouldn't go in the water. You could just take your surfboard back to the campsite. Harrison, the camp leader, will be serving dinner soon.

Then you see the speedboat.

It looks high-tech from a distance. But as it sputters closer to the shore, cutting a foamy white line through the gray ocean, gouges become visible in the fiberglass hull. Puffs of black smoke linger in the air behind it. A trail of leaked oil stretches all the way to the horizon.

The woman on board waves at you with a gloved hand. She's wearing a backpack and head-to-toe black padding, like an ice-hockey player. The outfit is too big for her. Maybe she borrowed it from somebody.

"Hey!" she yells. "You!"

You look back along the beach. There's still no one else around. She's talking to you.

"I'm not going to hurt you," the woman says. You take a step back. It hadn't occurred to you that she might be dangerous until she said that.

Her boat has nearly reached the shore.

"What do you want?" you ask.

The woman throws a square anchor overboard and climbs out of the boat. One leg of her pants is ripped. The skin underneath is blistered and pink, like she's been burned. She wades through the shallows toward you. Wet curly hair spills out over her shoulders.

"Do you have a phone?" she asks.

"No." You gesture at your wetsuit, which has no pockets.

She huffs in annoyance. "Are you one of the kids from the Karina Bay Surf Camp?"

You nod.

"What's your name, kid?"

If you say, "I'm Seth Ansari," turn to page 68.

If you say, "I'm Leah—what do you want?" turn to page 96.

06:04

Y ou sprint into the forest. At first it feels like running the wrong way on an escalator. You keep stumbling sideways. Soon your legs recover from the effects of the stun gun and you're going at full speed.

Harrison is a dangerous criminal. But he sent your friends to the lookout and was planning to follow them there, which probably means it's outside the blast radius. You have to hurry—at any moment the explosion could turn this part of the forest into a drifting cloud of ash.

As you flee deeper into the forest, you hear something. A faraway *whirring* sound. You stop, struggling to separate the noise from your desperate breaths and pounding heart.

It's a helicopter. Getting closer.

You look up. It could be the cops, here to save the day. Or it might be the people who planted the bomb making their escape. They won't want any witnesses. If they see you, Harrison might be the least of your worries.

Maybe they'll spot you through the canopy. Maybe they won't. Should you try to get their attention—or hide?

If you climb the nearest tree and try to attract the helicopter's attention, turn to the next page.

If you hide under the shrubbery, turn to page 79.

You scale the tree like a lizard. The adrenaline helps you find almost invisible hand- and footholds. You barely notice your aching shoulders and thighs as you climb from one branch to the next, twigs scraping your face, bark digging into your palms.

Soon your head breaks through the canopy. You can see the helicopter approaching through the darkening blue sky, silhouetted by the setting sun. You've never seen an aircraft like this up close—it's painted white, with massive landing skis and two rotors. One to keep it in the air, the other to steer, you guess. The markings on the sides are too far away to read.

"Hey!" you scream, waving. "Down here!"

There's no way they'll hear you over the whirling blades, and no sign that they've seen you. The helicopter comes closer. The wind from the rotors nearly knocks you over. You force yourself to keep your hands in the air as you balance on the branch.

"Hey!" you yell again. "Wait!"

A rope ladder unrolls out the side of the aircraft as it approaches. You've got their attention, whoever they are.

You stretch your arms up. The last rung of the ladder

swings by, almost out of reach. You just barely manage to snag it with one hand.

The ladder drags you out of the trees and into the air. You had assumed that the helicopter would slow down so you could climb up, but they seem to be in a hurry. All you can do is hang on.

Boom!

The earth erupts beneath you. Trees and clumps of dirt shoot up into the sky. You thought the helicopter was loud, but it's nothing compared to this. A hailstorm of tiny rocks pummels your back as a rush of hot air pushes you sideways. You swing under the helicopter, holding on to the ladder for dear life. It's a long way down. If you fall, you're dead.

The debris all rains back down into a smoking crater where the forest used to be. It looks like the mouth of a volcano. Your ears are ringing.

The rope ladder lurches upward, and you almost fall. Someone is pulling you up to the helicopter.

Your grip tightens as the ladder takes you higher and higher. When you've almost reached the open door, a man reaches out for you. He's dressed like he expects to be attacked by a pack of wild dogs. His arms are so padded he can hardly bend his elbows. His face is covered by a Plexiglass shield.

"Take my hand," he bellows.

He isn't dressed like a cop. But what else can you do?

You grab his outstretched glove and he hauls you into the helicopter. You're relieved to see four other people in the cabin, some in police uniforms. Agent Stacey is with them.

"Looks like you don't have to defuse the bomb, Gary," Stacey observes.

The guy in the padded suit smiles grimly. "Guess not."

"You escaped," you say.

Stacey nods. "Those two thugs weren't all that bright." She buckles you into a bench seat. "Your friends will be glad to see you," she says. "They're waiting at the lookout."

You rest your head back against the rubber pillow and close your eyes.

The helicopter wheels around and thunders through the fading light toward the lookout.

00:00

You survived! There are twelve other ways to escape the danger— try to find them all!

08:10

You dip your foot in the water and splash it around. "Hey!" you yell. "Ugly! Over here!"

The croc ignores you and keeps swimming toward Harrison. It opens its tremendous mouth, exposing a muscular tongue. The spikes on its back make it look like a burned meringue.

You jump into the waist-deep water. One foot squelches into the mud of the riverbed. The other lands on a flat stone. The crocodile still ignores you—

Until you bend down, snatch up the rock, and hurl it at the croc's yellow eye.

The stone misses the eyeball and bounces off the croc's tough hide. But now you have its attention. The croc whirls around to face you, hissing like a venomous snake.

You scramble back out of the water onto the stepping stones. Tail swooshing, the crocodile powers across the river like a runaway speedboat, heading right for you. You've saved Harrison's life, but what about yours?

You hop from one stepping stone to another. The rocks are slippery. One false step could send you crashing back down into the water, but you don't dare slow down.

At last you reach the shore. You're on dry land, where you have the advantage—

Or so you think. As you run into the trees, you hear the crocodile emerge from the water. It doesn't crawl or slither toward you—it actually gallops. You can hear its paws thumping the forest floor.

This thing can move, fast. Much faster than you. There's no hope of outrunning it.

Maybe you can outmaneuver it instead. It might not be able to change direction quickly—you could dive out of the way as it charges. Or maybe you should scramble up a tree. Crocs can't climb trees—can they?

If you head for the nearest tree, turn to page 94.

If you turn to face the croc so you can dodge as it attacks, turn to page 91.

05:12

You skirt around the rock and keep going, farther away from the cave. You hope you're not making a huge mistake. Any second now, that bomb will go off and turn this forest—and you—into compost.

The trail winds uphill to the lookout. You're getting closer—you can hear the ocean crashing on the shore. Maybe you'll make it beyond the blast radius in time.

Soon the trees thin out. The trail reaches the edge of a cliff and takes a sharp turn up a set of rotting wooden steps. Now you have the forest on your left and a sheer drop down to the ocean on your right. Hopefully—

Boom!

The explosion lights up the sky like a giant fireworks display. A terrifying pillar of smoke and debris grows larger and larger in the distance, getting closer and closer . . .

You sprint even faster up the steps, desperate to outrun the growing shockwave. You can feel the heat and light and noise building up and up behind you. Any second now, you'll be swallowed up by the blast.

Should you keep running? Or brace yourself against something?

If you grab a nearby tree and hold on tight, turn to page 112.
If you keep running, turn to page 16.

25:35

"It's this way," you say, and lead Stacey up the path. Even carrying your surfboard, it shouldn't take more than five minutes to get where you're going.

Stacey doesn't seem out of breath, despite the fact that she's jogging on a wounded leg. Is the burn even real?

"How many people are at the camp?" she asks.

"Uh . . ." You run through the list in your head. There's Pigeon, Neil, and Shelley—your friends—and three other kids whose names you haven't yet learned. Plus Harrison. But you're not sure you want Stacey knowing the exact number.

"Less than twenty," you say. Not really a lie. "Why?"

"That's two helicopter loads. Evacuation will be tricky."

"Evacuation? What are you talking about?"

"Everything I'm about to tell you is classified," she says. "If you share it with anyone you'll end up in detention."

You don't think she means detention like at school. You duck under the branches of a massive oak tree and keep walking. "So why are you telling me?"

"Because you need to understand how important this is. I've been undercover for two years, and if the next thirty minutes don't go perfectly, it will all have been wasted."

Ferns scrape at your legs. A gecko scampers across the path in front of you. You falter to avoid stepping on it.

"Keep moving," Stacey says.

You push on through the darkening forest. "Undercover where?" you ask.

"At an oil-drilling platform a quarter of a mile off the coast. We learned about the conspiracy years ago, but we couldn't prove anything, and I didn't know exactly where the bomb would be until today."

You can't have heard her right. "Did you say bomb?"

"Fifteen pounds of T4 plastic explosive," she says. "Enough to make a crater as big as a football field when it explodes—and I now know it's in the cave systems right next to your campsite."

You're starting to think that this must be a prank. "Why would anyone want to blow up a surf camp?"

"Something dangerous is in the water." Stacey sounds deadly serious. "I don't know what, but it means the company can't do any more offshore drilling. There's plenty of coal under this forest, so they're going to start mining here instead."

"But this is a national park."

"Not if it gets blown up. Then it's just dead land, and the government will be eager to sell it off."

"Won't it be obvious who planted the bomb?" you ask.

"They've falsified evidence to make it look like a rival company did it." Stacey checks her watch. "The bomb is scheduled to go off at sunset. I can disarm it, but—"

She suddenly tackles you to the ground. You drop your surfboard and cry out. She clamps a hand over your mouth.

"*Shhhhh*," she whispers, scanning the forest.

If you chose to take Stacey to the campsite, go to page 99.
If you've been leading her to the lookout, go to page 110.

09:32

"Hurry up!" Harrison keeps glancing at his watch. "The others will be wondering where we are."

You don't think that's very likely. Harrison's kind of annoying, and the others are probably glad to get a break from him. Pigeon in particular would welcome some unsupervised time.

"Did you hear that?" you ask.

Harrison doesn't break his stride. "Hear what?"

There it is again. A scraping, crackling noise. Like someone approaching through the forest. Maybe the other campers are coming back to look for you.

But when the figure emerges from the foliage up ahead, it's not one of the campers. It's another giant mercenary in a camouflage uniform.

He's not one of the two men who abducted Agent Stacey, but he looks exactly like them. You can hardly see his eyes under his tremendous brow. His bulky shoulders completely block the path.

"What is this?" Harrison sounds surprised, but not as much as he should.

The mercenary holds up two hands the size of dinner plates. "This is as far as you go."

"What are you talking about?" Harrison glances back

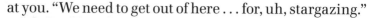

at you. "We need to get out of here . . . for, uh, stargazing."

"The plan has changed," the big guy says. "You're staying here."

You edge back toward the nearest cluster of trees.

Harrison glares at the man blocking the path. "You don't trust me?"

"If you leave, it will look like you knew what was coming." The brute spots you creeping away. "Hey!"

You turn to run, but the mercenary isn't alone. Another man jumps out of the trees and wrestles you to the ground. You struggle but you can't escape his grip. He's crushing your ribs.

Something tightens around your wrists. Handcuffs. No, it's some kind of plastic loop. You can see the other mercenary putting the same restraint on Harrison.

The two goons tie a coarse rope to a low-hanging tree branch, then wind the other end around your bound wrists. They attach Harrison to another tree, out of your reach. Now you can't run, and you can't help each other.

"This isn't necessary!" Harrison bellows. "We're not a threat to you! Untie us!"

The two goons completely ignore him. It's as if he's a ghost, invisible and inaudible to the living. They slip into the bushes and vanish, leaving you and Harrison standing opposite one another several feet apart, hands behind your backs.

As soon as they're out of sight, you start twisting your

arms and shoulders, trying to get the loop off your wrists. But it's no use. The plastic is tight and amazingly strong.

You try to break the branch you're tied to instead. But it's too thick. It might as well be an iron bar.

"Hey," you say.

Harrison won't meet your gaze. "It wasn't supposed to be like this," he mumbles. "You have to believe me. No one was supposed to get hurt."

His self-pity won't do you much good. Maybe there's another way you can get out of this.

If you took the rope from the equipment box back at the camp, go to page 45.

If you took the matches instead, turn to page 37.

03:03

You're almost at the lookout, but you have no hope of outrunning the explosion. It's rushing up behind you like a breaking wave sweeping toward the shoreline.

When it hits, it doesn't feel like getting thrown into the air. It doesn't seem like you're moving at all. Instead, it feels as though the whole world has shifted around you, the steps sliding away to your left and the ocean sweeping into focus on your right.

By the time you realize the blast has pushed you off the cliff, there's nothing you can do except scream as you plummet dizzily down to the jagged rocks and churning sea below.

Smash!

It takes all your willpower to keep your mouth closed as you crash down into the freezing water. You flounder, trying to get your head back above the surface.

Luckily, you're still wearing your wetsuit. Normal clothes would tangle you up and weigh you down. One of your flailing arms strikes a giant rock, hard enough to leave a bruise. You grab the rock to stop the water from dragging you back and forth. The rock stays steady. It's attached to the bottom of the cliff!

Gripping the rock with both hands, you haul yourself

up out of the roiling ocean and collapse, shivering. You lie against the cold stone worn smooth by centuries of waves. The cliffs seem intact. You hope that means your friends are OK at the lookout above.

The last echoes of the explosion die away, leaving just the hiss and gasp of the water.

00:00

You survived! There are twelve other ways to escape the danger— try to find them all!

You stay under the cover of the oak, watching fat drops of sea water slam into the dirt and fizzle out, leaving crusts of salt behind. It's dark, but you're not sure if night has actually fallen or if the clouds of steam have blocked out the setting sun.

The echoes of the blast are fading. The ocean roars as it floods back in to fill the void left by the explosion.

Snap! A root unravels on the other side of the tree. The force of the blast has damaged the oak too much. It's coming down!

Before you can get out of the way, the tremendous tree slams down on your back. You don't even have time to scream.

THE END.

Return to page 131 to try again!

I'll get Harrison," you shout. "You guys climb down the cliffs."

You don't wait to see if they follow your instructions. You run back toward the flames, squinting against the heat.

Harrison still hasn't moved. A puddle is growing under his helmet. Maybe he puked—or it could be blood.

You shake him by the shoulders, heedless of broken bones. "Harrison! Wake up!"

He doesn't move. You're going to have to carry him. But how? He's much bigger than you are. You haven't thought this through.

Pigeon grabs Harrison's hand. With shock, you realize that none of the others obeyed your order. They're all here, trying to help you and Harrison.

The flames spit and crackle. You take Harrison's other hand. Shelley and Neil lift his legs. Even divided by four, his weight is almost too much—but soon you're all carrying him back up the hill to the lookout, running like medieval soldiers with a battering ram.

You quickly reach the wooden safety rail and can go no farther.

"We can't climb down with him," you say.

"We can't leave him here," Pigeon says.

The flames lick closer and closer. It feels like plunging into a bath that hasn't had enough time to cool. You look around, but there's no way out. You're all trapped in a shrinking cage of fire.

At least you'll die with a clear conscience.

"Look!" Shelley shouts.

You turn toward the ocean. Through the flames you see something growing on the horizon. A tremendous wave—by far the biggest you've ever seen—is rushing at the shore, faster and faster. Soon it's so loud and close that you can't even hear the fire anymore.

"Down!" Shelley screams, which seems ridiculous. Surely the wave can't reach the lookout, all the way up here at the top of the cliff?

But the wave keeps getting taller, and suddenly it doesn't seem quite so ridiculous. The bomb must have set off some kind of oceanic quake. This isn't just a wave, it's a tsunami!

You throw yourself on the ground just in time. Water explodes over the edge of the lookout and slams down on top of you like a falling skyscraper. Had you been upright, the wave would have knocked you off your feet.

There's a deafening hiss as the sea water hits the fire. Steam fills the air. Half your body is unbearably hot. The rest is painfully cold. The water blends into the dirt under your face. You fight to keep your head above the mud.

Then it's over. The ocean recedes. Rivulets of water run away down the hill. The last of the ashes disintegrates. There's not a tongue of flame to be seen.

You spit out some muck. "Everyone OK?"

A chorus of groans surrounds you. Everyone's alive.

You lie on your back, catching your breath. Above you, the faded moon is coming into view.

00:00

You survived! There are twelve other ways to escape the danger—try to find them all!

01:02

You jump back just in time to avoid Stacey's clutching hand.

"No!" she cries, but it's too late for her to stop. She tumbles off the platform and falls to her death—

Except she doesn't. She falls only thirty or forty feet before she grabs some kind of tag on the strap of her backpack and pulls it. A pair of artificial wings burst out of her pack, and suddenly she's soaring like a hang-glider toward the shore.

The platform jolts under you again. You lose your balance and stagger closer to the edge. The more you try to back away along the tilting surface, the more you trip over your own feet. Suddenly you're stumbling off the edge of the platform and hanging in the air, three hundred feet over the churning ocean—

And then you fall. As you spin around and around, plummeting faster and faster, the last thing you see before you hit the water is Agent Stacey cruising away to safety.

THE END.

Return to page 60 to try again!

"**Y**eah, she gave me all the names and everything," you say. "If the bomb goes off, or something happens to her, you should have no trouble finding out who did it."

Hunt doesn't sound convinced. "Tell me what she told you exactly."

"I don't remember exactly," I say, "but I wrote it all down on a piece of paper."

"Well, read it out to me."

You're about to pretend you gave the paper to your camp leader, when the man with the big sunglasses—the man whose phone you're using—draws some kind of dart gun. A syringe sticks out of the barrel.

He takes aim at your face.

"Give me the paper," he says.

Shelley gasps. Neil yelps.

You should have seen this coming. "Hunt" clearly isn't a real cop, so the guy who called him must be part of the conspiracy.

"Give me the paper," the man says again.

You end the call so Hunt can't listen in. "I don't have it," you say.

"I'm not kidding," he says. "There's enough animal tranquilizer in this dart to knock out a megalodon."

"A what?" you ask.

"Give it to me!" he screams.

Pigeon is edging sideways. It looks like she's going to try to grab the guy from behind.

"I never made any notes," you say loudly. "I was bluffing."

The guy whirls around to face Pigeon. "Hey, get back!"

Pigeon hops backward and puts her hands up.

"All of you, get over there." The guy waves the dart gun in the direction of the cliff.

Everyone shuffles to the guardrail, including you. The gunman stays well out of reach. He has you trapped. He could march you all off the cliff if he wanted to.

"Last chance," he says. "Give me—"

A flash lights up the forest behind him.

"Down!" you yell, just in time.

Everyone drops to the ground—except the gunman, who hesitates, as if this might be some kind of trick. He's still on his feet when the shockwave hits.

Boom! Even this far away from the campsite, the explosion is hot, bright, and loud. It rolls right over you like a sudden sunburn. Dirt rains down on your back.

"No!" the gunman screams as the blast sweeps him off his feet—

And sends him flying over the guardrail. He vanishes into the darkness below the cliffs, screaming all the way.

Soon the heat fades and the echoes die away. When

the smoke clears, you climb to your feet. "Everyone OK?"

The words tickle in your throat. You choke, and cough up some black spit.

"I'm OK," Shelley says.

"Me too," Pigeon says.

"Yeah," Neil adds. "What happened to—"

He gets no farther. There's an ugly cracking sound.

"What was that?" Pigeon demands.

An ominous rumbling fills the air. The dirt shakes beneath you. The explosion must have damaged the underground caves.

"Earthquake!" Shelley yells.

And then the lookout starts to fall into the sea.

"The cliffs are collapsing!" you scream. "Run!"

The others are already sprinting back downhill to the forest. But the ground is crumbling around them. A deep crack opens up in the earth ahead, cutting all of you off from the mainland.

"Jump!" you yell.

The others sprint toward the widening chasm and leap over it, crash-landing on the other side.

You're last. The crevasse yawns before you. The earth tilts and slides under your feet.

You have a fifty-fifty chance of surviving this. You run and jump . . .

Go to page 105 . . .

. . . or to page 119.

You grab Stacey's hand and jump. You both fly off the edge of the oil-drilling platform, plummeting toward the deadly water below.

What were you thinking? It's too far down! You're both going to die—

And then she pulls a tab attached to her backpack.

Whumpf! An enormous pair of nylon wings explodes out of the pack, tearing through the fabric. You hurtle down and down, gaining speed. At the last second, Stacey pulls up. Your shoulder almost pops out of its socket as she takes your weight and swoops outward. Suddenly you're both soaring low over the ocean on Stacey's wings. Your feet practically skim the water as the collapsing oil rig shrinks into the distance behind you.

"Why didn't you tell me?" you shout.

"No time," Stacey says. "Lucky you trusted me."

Then she shifts her weight, banking left, carrying you to the safety of the beach.

00:00

You survived! There are twelve other ways to escape the danger—try to find them all!

06:04

There isn't much time. You grab a gnarled stick and plunge it into the remains of the fire. Yes! Under the ashes, the coals are still hot. The stick catches fire. You jam one end into the dirt and leave it to burn.

You run over to the biggest tent, which is a lightweight nylon dome. You tear the door right off, grab the foam rubber mattresses inside, and throw them out, along with books, portable coolers, backpacks—everything. When the tent is empty you unhook the guy ropes from the pegs and drag the whole thing over to the trees.

When you get there, you fling the big tent into the branches of the nearest tree. You snatch up the burning stick and run over to the dangling tent, trampling the mattresses in your haste. Shielding the flame with your hand, you hold the burning stick under the open door.

For a minute, nothing happens. Then the tent starts to bulge and stretch. It's filling up with hot air. It looks like this will work—but will it work fast enough?

When the tent looks ready to burst, you knot the guy ropes together and pull it away from the tree.

The tent, full of hot air, hangs above your head like a giant thought bubble. It actually floats! You've made your own hot air balloon. If you survive this, you're going to be so famous.

You wrap the ropes around your body. You're confident that they will take your weight, but it's hard to keep them away from the flame, while still keeping the torch under the tent door.

The improvized balloon is pulling harder and harder at the ropes. You hold on tight, and then . . .

Your feet leave the ground. Liftoff! Slowly but surely, the tent is taking you away. Soon it's too late to change your mind and let go. You're high enough now that the fall would break your legs.

Before long you're among the treetops, and then you're above them. The wind is stronger up here—it carries the tent sideways over the forest, toward the ocean. You fight to keep the guy ropes and the blazing stick steady.

Boom!

You happen to be looking down when the bomb goes off. It's like staring directly into the sun. For a moment you're blind. You can only hear the mighty roar and feel the ropes shuddering in your grip. The force of the blast knocks you in one direction while the wind pushes you the opposite way, fighting to fill the vacuum left by the explosion. Pebbles and dirt pelt your legs. You blink furiously, trying to get your sight back.

There's a sickening ripping sound from above you.

Your eyes recover in time to see a hole stretch open in the tent wall. A flying rock must have torn through the nylon.

The wind whistles through the tear as the hot air escapes. You're not gaining altitude anymore. In fact, you seem to be falling.

And the forest below is on fire. The blast scattered enough superheated ash into the trees that the dry leaves and branches are ablaze.

The heat washes over you and dries out your eyeballs. Your kicking legs are getting closer and closer to the flames. You're getting smoked like a pig on a spit. It's looking less and less likely that you'll reach the sea.

The tear in the tent has left it lopsided. It's turning around in a slow circle. Maybe you could steer by pulling the guy ropes. But you'd have to drop the burning stick, which will make the tent descend even faster.

If you drop the stick and try to steer the tent to safety, turn to page 35.
If you hold on and wait for the tent to carry you over the ocean, turn to page 59.

You fling out a desperate hand to grab the surfboard, which is still wedged in the dirt. You manage to get a grip, but the board is slippery. You dangle over the crater, legs kicking helplessly as you fight for a firmer hold with your other hand.

The dirt shifts. The board creaks as it comes loose of its moorings. Suddenly you're tumbling into the crater, along with the board and several clumps of earth!

It's a long way down. A fatal drop. But the wall of the crater isn't quite vertical. There's a slight slope, leading to the bowl-shaped basin.

As you fall, you snatch the board out of the air and press it to your feet.

This seems too crazy to possibly work, but when the board hits the dirt wall, the fins snap off immediately and the board slides. Not as smoothly as on water, but it's just steady enough that you don't get thrown off. Whooping like a lunatic, you hurtle down the side of the crater, the surfboard skipping and slipping beneath your feet.

After a terrifying ride, the ground levels out. You've reached the bottom of the crater. You throw yourself off before you reach the sharp rocks, landing on warm dirt. The board grinds to an abrupt halt a few feet away.

You lie on your back, watching the smoke clear. You can hear a helicopter droning in the distance. With any luck it's the cops, here to rescue Agent Stacey—and to pick up your friends from the lookout.

But it could be a while before anyone comes looking for you here. You look up at the wall of the crater. Better get climbing.

00:00

You survived! There are twelve other ways to escape—try to find them all!

A sharp turn is coming up. Harrison will have to edge around a big rock that mostly blocks the path. Once he's on the other side, it'll take him a minute to realize you're not following.

You wait for him to squeeze around the big rock, and then you sprint back the way you came.

Another trail splits off from this one. You almost didn't see it—a shroud of hanging vines mostly conceals the entrance. You pull them aside and duck through. Maybe Harrison will run right past.

"Hey!" he yells in the distance. "Where are you?"

You don't stop, but the twists and bends of the trail get tighter and tighter, forcing you to slow down. Harrison is crashing through the brush somewhere behind you. Will he see the hidden path, or spot you in the foliage?

There! A narrow cave between two gigantic stones. He won't see you in there. You slip into the shadows and hold your breath.

Harrison's footsteps get closer and closer—

And then they fade. He's gone past the trail without seeing your footprints. You let the air out of your lungs.

It's not quite pitch black in the cave. It's lit by a faint red glow. You turn around, looking for the source.

It's a small LED readout, attached to a tangle of wires and a lump of what looks like orange clay. A code is printed on the side: T4.

The screen says 05:20.

Now 05:19.

You've found the bomb.

You stare at it in silent horror for a moment. You have five minutes and seventeen seconds before this place turns into a smoldering crater. Is that enough time to get out of range?

Maybe not. But there aren't very many buttons or wires. Perhaps it wouldn't be too hard to defuse the bomb.

If you run for your life, turn to page 115.

If you try to defuse the device, turn to page 101.

ou stagger and stumble away from the burning tree. It's hard to see the trail through the smoke, but you make your own path by breaking branches and trampling shrubs. Your stomach muscles ache from all the coughing. The bitter stench makes you want to throw up.

You need to be sure you're headed away from the bomb. But the forest looks the same in every direction. You're hopelessly lost.

"Harrison?" you rasp. "Where are you?"

No reply. You hope the mercenaries didn't hear you.

Boom!

Go to page 139.

02:06

You let go of the stick. It plummets into the flames below.

With less heat flooding into it—and more in the air outside—the tent is falling faster and faster. You figure you have a minute at the most before you crash.

There's a dark patch to your left. Nothing is on fire over there, so far. The ground is strewn with bits of camping gear and forest debris from the explosion, but there are no trees to burn. You yank the guy rope in your left hand. The tent tips and starts a slow circle downward to safety.

Except it's not safe. You're falling way too fast now. Even if you make it out of the fire's reach, you'll still crush every bone in your body when you hit the ground—

Then you see something that could save your life.

You wrench down on the guy rope in your right hand. The floating tent leans the other way but doesn't change direction as much as you'd hoped.

The ground rushes up to meet you. At the last second you let go of the ropes, hoping you won't overshoot your target—

Wham! You slam down onto the tattered camping mattress. Torn scraps of melted rubber stick to your legs. Of all the mattresses you threw out of the tent earlier, this is the thickest, but it still feels like hitting a brick wall. You groan, lying on your stomach on the smoldering rubber as the tent flies over you and settles nearby like a jellyfish washed up on the beach.

It's like reaching dry land after hours of surfing. Your legs are so wobbly and sore that it's a while before you can stand. You look back at the tremendous crater under a column of steam and smoke. On the far edge of it you can see the lookout perched atop the cliffs.

You start trudging around the edge of the crater. It's time to join your friends.

00:00

You survived! There are twelve other ways to escape the danger—try to find them all!

07:02

You dropped the box of matches when the mercenary grabbed you. You can't reach it with your hands, but you might be able to kick it over to Harrison. You stretch out one foot for a practice swing.

"What are you doing?" Harrison asks.

"These restraints are made of plastic," you say. "Maybe we can melt them. Here, catch." You kick the matchbox. It bounces across the dirt and lands at Harrison's feet. When he crouches, it's just within his reach.

You can feel the seconds ticking away. The bomb could go off at any moment. "Hurry," you say.

Harrison fumbles with the box for a while behind his back and eventually gets it open. He digs out a match and strikes it against the side of the box.

It doesn't flare. He tries again. Nothing happens.

You're about to tell him to toss it over to you so you can try, when the match bursts into flames. Harrison yelps and drops the match, but it doesn't matter. The loop around his wrists has already caught fire, and it disintegrates almost immediately. Harrison is free.

But you might have created more problems than you solved. As Harrison rubs his burned skin, the fire spreads from the brush at his feet to the leaves of the tree you're tied to. Branches crackle. Boughs smoulder. Harrison backs away from the burning tree.

"Give me the matches!" you cry.

Harrison snatches up the matchbox and throws it at you too hard. You can't move your hands to catch it, so it flies past and lands on the ground out of reach.

"Harrison!" you shout, but he's already running away from the fire.

You try to reach the matchbox with your feet, but it's not going to happen. Your legs aren't long enough.

The fire snakes along the branch toward you, spitting hungry sparks. The smoke stings your eyes. You might burn to death before the bomb goes off—

Snap! Your wrists are suddenly free. The plastic loop has softened enough from the heat to break.

You try to crawl away from the tree, but the smoke has made you dizzy. Somehow you end up facedown in the mud.

The mercenaries left you here, so you must still be in the blast radius. Dizzy or not, you'll have to run for it . . .

You can see a ditch and what looks like a log only a few feet away. Maybe you should take shelter instead.

If you crawl into the ditch, turn to page 73.

If you get to your feet and run as far away as you can, turn to page 34.

The thought that your friendly camp leader is part of a violent corporate conspiracy is ridiculous. "Just what I told you," you say. "She didn't show me any ID, but she sounded serious."

Harrison visibly relaxes. "Well, sometimes people play tricks on kids. Come on. Let's head for the lookout."

You follow him as he checks the last two tents, making sure no one has been left behind. Then he hops over a low fence and jogs into the trees. You don't have any trouble crossing the fence; it's designed to stop cars, not people. But you're falling behind Harrison, who's already hurrying up a narrow path into the forest.

"Wait for me," you say.

Harrison slows down a little. "Come on," he says.

"What's the rush?" you ask, pushing a branch aside. "The stars will be there all night."

He doesn't look at you. "I don't want the others to worry about us."

That makes sense, but the way he says it leaves you feeling uneasy. Maybe Harrison is up to something.

If you keep following Harrison to get to your friends, turn to page 13.
If you try to lose him in the forest, turn to page 32.

0201

You grab the nearest rock with both hands. One hand misses. But the other manages to get a firm grip. You find yourself dangling from one hand over the mouth of the crater. Success!

But how are you going to get down? The walls of the crater are smooth and so steep they may as well be vertical. A jagged clutter of blasted stones fills the basin far below. If you fall, you'll break every bone in your body as you bounce down to the bottom.

You'll have to climb up instead, back over the remains of the ditch and into the safety of the forest. You heave yourself up—

The rock you're holding onto pops out of the dirt like a rotten tooth.

Soil showers your face. You scrabble for another handhold, but it's too late. You're falling down, down, down, rolling toward the sharp rocks at the bottom of the crater . . .

Crunch!

THE END.

Go back to page 37 to try again!

0 4 5 9

You paddle over to where the big fan is bobbing on the water, grab the edge, and try to climb up on top of it. But it capsizes immediately, flipping you back down into the ocean.

Your heart is lodged in your throat. You can't see the shark coming but you can feel it, rising up beneath you, jaws open wide . . .

You grab the fan again, this time reaching as far over it as possible, gripping the metal grill near the center. The fan rocks from side to side as you crawl up onto it, but doesn't tip over.

Wobbling like a hula hoop champion, you stand in the middle. The fan takes your weight, but it's far from steady. If you lose your balance, you'll fall in and the shark will get you.

You choke back a scream as a chipped fin as big as a windsurfing sail rises above the waves and cruises past the floating fan. You can see the shimmering outline of the shark below, surrounded by the cloud of tiny parasites that follow it around and feed off its scraps.

It doesn't seem to see you. The shark sinks into the darkness of the ocean and vanishes.

You let out a shaky breath. You can't go back in the

water. So without the hovercraft, how will you and Stacey get to shore? You're stuck under an oil rig full of hostile—

Smash! The giant shark explodes out of the darkness beneath you and slams its jaws closed around the fan. You scream and topple sideways into the cold sea.

For a moment you're blind and deaf. You thrash around in the water, trying to work out which way is up.

Your head breaches the surface, and is immediately submerged again. You fight your way back up. It's like trying to stay afloat in a hurricane.

When you break through into the daylight you see the creature flailing like a trout on a hook, its tail flinging sheets of water left and right.

The fan is still stuck in its mouth.

The shark can't chew through the steel. Its gigantic teeth are wedged in the grill—it can't spit the fan out. This is your chance to swim to the shore.

You launch off the pylon and freestyle to the beach, leaving the choking leviathan behind. Salt water slaps your face. Your feet are numb in the cold, but the adrenaline keeps them kicking.

The beach comes into view from behind the cliffs. It's about a quarter of a mile to the shore. Your personal record for swimming a distance like that was eight minutes. You feel like you're about to cut that time in half. You're so scared of the shark that you're swimming almost as fast as you can run.

You risk a look back. There's the oil rig on the horizon. You're already a long way away from it—

But the shark is catching up to you.

A huge fin cuts through the water, heading for your legs. As the monstrous head approaches the surface, you can see that the creature's mouth is closed. It has managed to spit out the fan—or swallow it. Those ancient eyes are looking right at you, getting closer and closer.

The jaws open wide, exposing a ring of teeth like kitchen knives. You scream—

Boom!

An explosion rips out from the shoreline. The bomb near the camp site must have gone off. Trees and rocks shoot up from the forest. The sea water kicks up and fizzles into vapor. You're flung backward. as if by a massive wave, toward the shark's open mouth—

But the blast knocks the shark back, too, rolling it sideways in the water. You miss the mouth and crash into a gray wall. You're so dizzy that it's not until you touch the giant gills that you realize you're up against the shark's sandpapery flank.

The water swirls around you, heated by the explosion. It's like being trapped in a washing machine. The shark is stunned but alive. Its titanic jaws open and close like those of a goldfish.

You're still three hundred feet from the shore. You

could swim for it. But what if the shark recovers and catches up to you?

You spit out some salt water and take a deep breath. You don't have a choice—

Or do you?

If you swim to the beach, turn to page 116.

If you climb up on the stunned shark's back, turn to page 51.

You dropped the rope when the mercenary grabbed you, but it's still within reach. You stretch out your foot, snag the coil, and drag it back toward you.

"We're already tied up," Harrison says. "How is more rope going to help?"

"I'm not strong enough to break this branch," you say. "But with your help, maybe I can."

You loop the rope around the branch. It's hard with your hands stuck behind your back, but eventually you manage it. You toss both ends to Harrison.

Every second counts. "Pull!" you yell.

You heave on the branch as Harrison pulls on the rope. The plastic tie cuts into your wrists. Your hands swell up. The branch bends, but doesn't break.

"It's not working," Harrison grunts.

"Pull harder!"

Sweat pours down your face. The branch creaks behind you—and then cracks.

"Yes!" you cry. You keep tugging on the branch until it rips off the tree and hits the ground. The rope slips off. You pull your wrists under your legs so your hands are bound in front of you, rather than behind.

"Hurry!" Harrison urges.

You run over to him and fumble with the knots behind his back. The mercenaries knew what they were doing. The restraints are very tight.

"There!" Finally the rope comes loose. Harrison is free of the branch, although the plastic tie still holds his wrists together.

"Which way?" you ask.

"I think—"

Boom!

Go to page 139.

You race up the trail to the lookout, keeping your eyes on the ground. Sharp rocks and sticks scatter the dirt. One false step could leave you bleeding and limping. In a forest with a bomb hidden somewhere in it, every second counts. Soon you can hear voices.

"Never?" Pigeon is saying. "Like, never ever?"

What's she doing up at the lookout? Shouldn't she be at camp?

"No. I've never read *The Dreaded Ones*," Shelley says, sounding like her patience is wearing thin. "Why is that so difficult to believe?"

"But everyone's read that book."

"I haven't," Neil interjects.

"I meant every girl has read it," Pigeon says.

"You assumed I haven't read it just because I'm a boy?" Neil sounds offended.

"I assumed you haven't read it because you just said so!"

Their discussion is cut short when you burst out of the forest, nearly crashing into Shelley. The area's not much more than a patch of gravel, a small parking lot, and a public toilet. A wooden handrail stops anyone from falling three hundred feet into the ocean below.

"There's-a-bomb-at-the-campsite-and-a-federal-agent-has-been-kidnapped!" you pant.

A man sitting on a park bench nearby looks over at you in alarm. But your friends just seem confused.

"Wha . . . ?" Neil says.

"Someone planted a bomb," you say, still puffing from your run up the hill, "near the campsite. A federal agent told me about it—right before she was abducted."

You look around. All the kids from camp are here, plus the man on the bench, who's punching numbers into his phone. But there's no sign of the camp leader.

"Where's Harrison?" you ask.

"He sent us up here to do some stargazing," Shelley says skeptically. "He said he'd be right behind us."

"We need to call the police. Does anyone have a phone?"

"I do," the man on the bench says. He's a tall, skinny guy with big sunglasses. He stands up and holds out his phone. "Here, I've got the cops on the line."

"Thanks." You take the phone from him. "Hello?"

"This is Detective Sergeant Fred Hunt. Can we start with your name and date of birth, please?"

"We don't have time," you say. "There's a bomb near the Karina Bay Surf Camp. It's—"

"The bomb squad is already en route," Hunt says. "All civilians are at a safe distance. Name and date of birth, please."

You tell him.

"Thank you. Now tell me about this agent who was

kidnapped. Did you get her name?"

"Agent Stacey."

"First name, or last?"

"I'm not sure."

"OK. Did she give you any information? Anything we could use to find the perpetrators?"

"She said the bomb was planted by a mining company who want to get to the coal under the campsite."

"Did she name the company?" Hunt asks urgently. "Or anyone involved? Did she show you any evidence?"

It sounds like he doesn't believe Agent Stacey. And come to think of it, she never showed you any identification proving she was from the authorities.

You're about to reply when you hear someone yelling in the background on the other end of the phone, "Don't tell them anything!" before abruptly falling silent.

It's hard to tell over the fuzziness of the phone line, but it sounds like Stacey.

"I want to know everything she told you," Hunt says, as though nothing happened. "Word for word."

Is Stacey with Hunt? If so, why would she tell you not to say anything? Aren't they on the same side?

Maybe Agent Stacey isn't a real agent—or maybe she is, and Hunt is one of the guys who kidnapped her. Who do you trust?

If you tell Hunt the truth, turn to page 97.

If you bluff and pretend Stacey told you everything, turn to page 23.

"**Y**ou know!" you say. "About the bomb!"

"There is no bomb," Harrison says. He's not laughing now. Veins stand out of his neck.

"That's why you sent everyone on a stargazing trip this early in the day," you say. "That's how you know the agent is a woman, even though I didn't say so."

"Do you know how crazy you sound right now?" Harrison pulls a phone out of his pocket. It's old and chunky, with a keypad instead of a touchscreen.

"Did they threaten you?" you ask. "The mining company that planted the bomb? Or did they offer you money?"

Harrison holds his phone out to you. "Take it."

You hesitate. "Why?"

"So you can call the police," he says. "They'll tell you you're being paranoid."

He's wearing shorts and a tight polo shirt. There's nowhere he could be hiding a weapon. But he is bigger than you.

If you take the phone and call the cops, turn to page 120.
If you pretend to believe Harrison, turn to page 86.

02:00

You stick your fingers into the gills and haul yourself up the shark's flank. Its skin is as scratchy as a cat's tongue. The shark is starting to wake up—its spine bends left and right like a tree in a strong wind. Wondering whether this is all just a bizarre dream, you climb up on the shark's back and grab hold of its enormous fin.

You're pretty sure the shark can't see you up here—and because you're out of the water, it can't smell you or hear your heartbeat. You're safe. As safe as it's possible to be while standing on the back of a sixty-foot shark.

You stare at the bombed-out beach. It's a wreck, the muddy puddles filled with blackened husks of trees. Ash rains down from the sky.

Your friends at the camp must be dead. Nothing could have survived that blast. There's a painful twisting sensation in your chest.

The shark rolls over.

You barely have time to scream before you're plunged into the sea. You keep your arms wrapped tightly around the massive fin as the shark drags you under.

Hundreds of years ago, sailors used to be "keel-hauled"—tied up and dragged under their own ships as punishment for crimes. That's what this feels like. Your lungs burn. Water pounds your eardrums and floods up your nose. You hold your breath until the shark completes the barrel roll and you surface on the other side. You cling desperately to the fin as the shark rights itself.

Having failed to dislodge you, the shark starts swimming for the shore. It's not deep enough for it to descend, so it thrashes on the surface like an electric eel. You grip the fin tightly as the shark swims around in wild circles.

You keep your feet apart and your hips low. You're surfing on a giant shark. This is insane.

With a scraping, grinding sound, the shark comes to a sudden halt. You lose your grip on the fin and hurtle through the air, spinning around and around, and then—

Splash! You hit the water and immediately slam into the sand beneath it. The water is less than two feet deep.

You sit up, spluttering, in time to see the shark chomp its mammoth jaws at you . . .

But it can't reach. It's too big, and the water's too shallow. In its desperation to reach you, the shark has beached itself like a lost whale. It gasps, eyes rolling. It's suffocating.

You crawl away, dragging yourself up out of the shallows. You collapse on the beach among the charred sticks and rubble. You're safe.

"Hey!"

You turn your head. Shelley is sprinting across the

beach toward you. She survived! The others are running right behind her.

In the distance, the shark squirms and wriggles. At first you think it's trying to get to you, but it's not. It slides backward farther and farther until there's enough water under it to turn around. Then it swims out into the open sea and disappears.

The ocean looks safe and peaceful once more.

00:00

You survived! There are twelve other ways to escape the danger— try to find them all!

08:10

You sprint across the stepping stones, desperate to reach Harrison before the croc does. Even though the creature is huge—maybe twenty feet long—it moves amazingly quickly through the now-murky water. There's every chance it will reach Harrison before you do. But it's too late to change your mind.

"Grab my hand!" you shout as you get closer and closer to Harrison, who's screaming like a terrified monkey.

He reaches out and you grab his wrist, hauling him up on the stepping stones. You both run the rest of the way across to the forest, shoes squelching, clothes dripping.

But the crocodile doesn't give up. It slides up the river-bank like a nightmare come to life and bounds into the trees after you. Maybe you could outrun it on an Olympic racetrack, but not here. The forest, with its muddy trails and tripping hazards, is the croc's domain.

The trail forks up ahead on either side of a deep ditch. You go right. Harrison goes left. You wonder if he knows something you don't, and selfishly hope the croc follows him.

It doesn't. You can hear the thudding of its paws against the dirt behind you. The beast is catching up.

And now you see why it chose to run after you rather

than Harrison. A rockfall has blocked the trail up ahead. You could scramble over the pile of stones, but probably not fast enough.

You turn around. Harrison watches helplessly from the other side of the ditch. He's out of reach. You're on your own.

The rampaging croc runs at you, jaws frothing.

If you took the matches from the box back at the camp, turn to page 125.
If you took the rope instead, turn to page 128.

The sand squeaks under your feet as you sprint toward the trees. But you don't want to go too far, since the explosion might pick up rocks from the forest floor and throw them around like bullets.

The massive oak tree is just ahead. You hope it's strong enough to withstand the blast.

You duck around it just in time.

The bomb explodes in the ocean behind you, filling the sky with sizzling droplets and clouds of steam. The sand erupts like a volcano, flinging hot debris past your hiding place. The sound hits you a split second later—a tremendous *KABOOM* that shakes the ground beneath your feet.

The mighty oak groans, straining under the pressure from the blast. It tilts a little but seems to hold. Maybe you should get out from under it—but the echoes of the explosion haven't yet died away, and suddenly it's raining hot water. The sea is coming back down, and it will burn you.

If you leave the shelter of the tree, turn to page 90.
If you stay where you are, turn to page 18.

ou duck into the bushes, feeling Stacey's eyes on you. You wonder if she thinks you're a coward.

After a few seconds the two big men emerge from the trees on the other side of the clearing.

"Which trigger went off?" one asks.

"That one," the other says, pointing at the bushes you're hiding behind. "I'll check on the feed."

The first guy walks in your direction. Where is the laser trip wire? What if he sees you?

You're paralyzed, deciding whether to run or stay.

Too late. The big man's ice-blue eyes focus on you. "Hey!" he roars. "It's the kid!"

You scramble backward through the shrubbery, but not fast enough. The man takes three big strides on his long legs, reaches down through the leaves with a massive arm, and grabs the collar of your wetsuit.

"Gotcha!" he says, lifting you up.

Whack! Something hits him. He lets go of you and collapses.

You fall to the ground beside him and watch in amazement as Agent Stacey turns to face the other mercenary. Somehow she's gotten free of her bonds, crossed the clearing, and knocked your captor out.

The other guy swings a meaty fist at her. She ducks under the blow, grabs his arm, and flings him over her shoulder in some kind of judo throw. He hits the dirt with a thud and doesn't get up again.

Stacey digs through his pockets until she finds a phone. Her backpack is lying at the edge of the clearing. She grabs it and puts it on.

"But you were tied up," you stammer.

"They thought I was. Come on." Stacey hauls you to your feet. "We have to get back out to the oil platform."

"Wait," you say. "We?"

She nods. "I can't pilot the hovercraft by myself."

"Hovercraft?!"

Go to page 133.

02:06

You keep the burning stick held high, flooding the floating tent with as much hot air as possible. But you're losing altitude fast. There's not much temperature difference between the air inside the balloon and the air outside it, so it's struggling to stay aloft.

The cliffs are about fifty feet away. After that you'll be over the open ocean, where the water will break your fall and you can swim back to the shore.

But the trees beneath you are getting closer and closer. Hitting them at this speed would be fatal.

You're not going to make it to the ocean. A tree rushes up to meet you. At the last second you drop your makeshift torch and reach out, hoping to grab a branch before you crash into the trunk—

Whack!

You know nothing more.

THE END.

Return to page 120 to try again!

"OK, OK!" You walk over to the door, unlock it, and open it.

One of the security guards drags you out to the deck. You're sweating under your wetsuit. What if you've made a terrible mistake? They might kill you both.

The man in the suit doesn't even look at you. He's watching through the window as the numbers on the screen tick down.

00:02.

00:01.

00:00.

"Well," he says, "that's it."

Nothing happens at first. Then the screens which were monitoring the camp site go black. A message pops up: NO SIGNAL.

A distant rumble fills the air. It gets louder and louder until the floor starts to shake beneath your feet.

"Get down!" Stacey cries.

You flop to the metal floor. The man in the suit yells something, but you're not sure what. One of the security guards slips over and lands headfirst on the ground next to you. His eyes roll back. A pink bruise swells up on his temple.

The thunder fades. If your friends were in the tents, they're dead now. You feel sick.

"What happened?" the boss demands. "The explosion wasn't supposed to affect the rig."

"The mercenaries must have laid the charges in the wrong place," one of the security guards says.

"Speaking of laying charges," Agent Stacey says, "did I mention that you're all under arrest?"

The boss points a stubby finger at her. "You are in no position to—"

A deafening creak interrupts him. The whole mining platform is groaning.

"Is it supposed to do that?" you ask.

No one gets the chance to answer you. The whole structure lurches sideways. The floor tilts to a violent angle, throwing you and everyone else against the shipping container.

"The rig is collapsing!" a security guard shouts.

The boss herds his security people toward the stairs. "Go, go, go!"

Agent Stacey wipes the blood off her face and drags you to your feet. "Come on!"

You follow her. It's pandemonium on the main deck. People run back and forth all over the platform, yelling confusing orders at one another. The whole rig has tilted, leaving the walkways at crazy angles. Stairs are vertical, ladders are horizontal. One of the support struts under the platform must be sinking into the ocean floor.

The boss and his security team have forgotten all about you and Stacey. They're scaling a wobbling ladder to a helipad. The helicopter is sliding sideways across the landing pad as the oil platform tilts more and more.

Other people are jumping off the edge of the platform into the water. Because of the way the oil rig is shifting and tilting, from this corner it's only a thirty or forty foot drop into the ocean.

"This way," Stacey yells, heading the other way. She runs up the slope and scales a flight of stairs. Why is she going up? Shouldn't you both be trying to get off the rig as quickly as possible?

If you jump into the water with the other workers, turn to page 69.
If you follow Stacey, turn to page 71.

08:04

You grab the steel cable. It's somehow slippery and rough at the same time. How did Stacey climb this so easily?

The underside of the rig looks impossibly high up— but the sputtering of tranquilizer guns above gives you an adrenaline rush. Another dart hits the hovercraft. You can't see where the shot came from, and you don't stick around to find out. You start climbing the cable.

It's a tough climb. The steel fibers burn your hands. You're not making much headway . . .

Until you accidentally kick the harpoon gun.

The cable starts to retract. The gun whizzes up toward you. You let go of the cable just in time to avoid getting your fingers sucked into the mechanism—but you catch hold of the gun barrel instead. It drags you up and up to the underside of the oil rig until it thunks against the harpoon embedded in the steel.

The hovercraft starts to float away below, now that the gun isn't connecting it to the rig.

You hang there for a moment. No one can see you, so the gunshots have stopped. But you can't dangle up here forever. Your shoulders and biceps already ache.

The hatch Stacey climbed through is right above you.

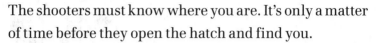

The shooters must know where you are. It's only a matter of time before they open the hatch and find you.

There's no choice but to push the hatch open and pull yourself up.

When you climb through into the daylight, you find yourself on a massive steel platform, crisscrossed with ladders, walkways, and staircases. It's a maze. You see Stacey running along some scaffolding above, but you can't figure out how to get to her.

Ping! Another ballistic dart ricochets off a handrail right near your arm. The shooter, perched in a distant lookout, starts reloading her tranquilizer rifle. You turn and run up the nearest staircase, desperate to get out of sight.

A PA system crackles and whines. "Attention crew. We have two wanted criminals on board."

The voice echoes around the platform, bouncing back at you from all possible angles. It takes you a minute to realize he's talking about you.

"Return to your quarters," the voice continues, "and lock your doors while security apprehends the intruders. If you see them, pull the nearest fire alarm."

You circle around a massive stack of barrels, trying to break the shooter's line of sight. You find yourself face to face with a terrified-looking man in overalls and a hard hat.

He reaches for a red handle on the wall.

You raise your hands. "Don't! Please—I'm not a criminal! I'm just a kid!"

The guy pulls the handle. An alarm shrieks as he sprints the other way.

You flee up another flight of stairs toward a row of shipping containers, packed side by side. Your bare feet clang against the metal as you climb. When you get closer to the shipping containers, you realize they're actually being used as rooms—windows and doorframes have been cut into them.

Ping! A dart strikes the corrugated wall near your head. Forget about getting tranquilized—a shot like that could take out your eyeball. You need somewhere to hide.

You turn to the closest shipping container and try the door. Locked. You run to the next container and pull another handle.

The door opens. You dive through, pull it closed behind you, and lock it.

The container is full of computers. Cables trail from droning towers and crackling speakers to big antennae and phones with hundreds of buttons. A dozen monitors show people moving about the oil platform—

And the campsite. You can see the tents, the clothesline, the smoldering remains of the bonfire. The whole time you and your friends were having fun at surf camp, someone was watching you through hidden cameras.

You can't see your friends on the screens. They could be inside the tents—or maybe up at the lookout.

Someone tries to open the door, but it's still locked. There's a table up against the window—you duck beneath it so no one can see you from outside.

"Hey," a muffled voice says. "Kid."

You stay out of sight, heart pounding.

"I know you're in there." It sounds like the same guy who called you a criminal over the PA. "You have thirty seconds to come out—or your friend dies."

Leaning slightly out from under the table, you risk a peek out the window. Behind it stands a gray-haired man with a cleft chin and floppy jowls. He wears a charcoal suit, the shoulders and sleeves tailored to his frame. He has the look of a boss—a mean one.

He's not alone. There are two uniformed security guards—and Agent Stacey. She's on her knees. One of the guards is holding her by the back of her neck. Her nose is bleeding.

"You now have ten seconds," the man in charge says.

Your breaths get tighter. Neither the boss nor the guards seem to have any weapons. But Stacey doesn't look like she's in a position to defend herself.

"Eight seconds," the boss continues.

"Don't do it," Stacey says. "You have to stop the—"

The security guard clamps a hand over her mouth.

"Five," the man says, as though she hadn't spoken.

Your mind is racing. If you stay, they'll kill Stacey. But if you leave, they might kill both of you.

"Four," the man says.

Why does he want you out of the room so badly? And what was Stacey trying to tell you?

You follow her gaze to one of the computer monitors. Instead of a video feed, it has a timer, counting down to something. And some text: PRESS ANY KEY TO CANCEL DETONATION.

The timer ticks over from 00:29 to 00:28.

"Three," the man says.

If you touch the keyboard nearest the screen, you'd definitely be sacrificing Agent Stacey's life to maybe stop the explosion, and maybe save your friends.

"Two," the man says.

If you walk out of the room and save Stacey's life, turn to page 60.
If you touch a key on the keyboard, turn to page 77.

28:43

"All right, Seth. My name is Agent Stacey," the woman says. "I've come to warn everyone at the camp—you're all in danger."

Her eyes are unreadable behind her sunglasses.

"What kind of danger?" you ask.

"I'll explain on the way."

She turns toward the long, spiky grass in front of the forest. Two paths are visible. The left one goes directly to the campsite. The right one trails through the forest and eventually leads to a lookout on top of the cliffs.

"What's the quickest way to the campsite?" she asks.

Your gaze falls on her battered boat. Small circular holes are scattered among the scratches and dents. "Are those bullet holes?"

"My GPS got broken when I escaped," she says, ignoring your question. "I need you to show me the fastest way to the camp from here right now."

If this woman is dangerous, leading her to camp could put your friends at risk. You could take her up the other path to the lookout instead. Lots of tourists will be around there. You'll be safe.

Do you lead her left to the camp or right to the lookout? Make your choice, and turn to page 10.

You ignore Stacey and run into the crowd of mining workers. They're grabbing flotation devices from an emergency equipment box bolted to the floor. If any of them notices you—the "criminal" they were supposed to be watching out for a moment ago—they don't say anything.

You grab a life jacket from the box and pull it over your head. All sorts of whistles, lights, and buckles hang from it, but eventually you find the strap that goes around your waist. You connect the clips.

"What about the megalodon?" someone yells.

"We'll have to risk it," someone else replies.

You're about to ask what a "megalodon" is when the worker in front of you pulls a cord. His life jacket inflates with a hiss. You do the same. *Whoosh!* The jacket swells up around your neck. You can barely see over the top of it—you must be wearing it backward.

The worker jumps off the platform and splashes down into the ocean. You realize you've reached the front of the line. You turn your life jacket around while you wait for him to swim out of the way. Then you take a deep breath and jump.

You fall for a heart-stopping second before you crash

down into the freezing water. The vest hits you in the face almost hard enough to hurt. The light flickers on. It must be designed to react with water.

You paddle sideways so the next person can jump in—

And then the oil platform lets out an ominous groan.

"It's coming down!" someone shrieks.

The concrete pylons crack. Steel ropes snap and support struts bend. You swim as fast as you can toward the other workers, floating at a safe distance—

But it's too late. A million tons of oil platform crash down on top of you.

THE END.

Go back to page 63 to try again!

02:08

You run up to meet Stacey at the top of the stairs. She grabs your hand and drags you past the shipping containers to a massive cargo elevator. The doors are already open.

"Will this thing still work?" you ask.

"I have no idea. But we don't have time for the stairs." She steps into the elevator and slams her hand down on the button. An alarm buzzes. You barely have time to jump in before the doors roll closed.

Because the oil platform is sliding into the sea, the elevator is crooked. You're not just riding it up, you're riding it up and sideways. The car grinds against the shaft, shooting sparks.

"Why are we going up?" you ask. "Shouldn't we be trying to get down to the hovercraft?"

"That hovercraft is about to be buried under a million tons of metal and concrete," she says. "But I have another way to get off."

The elevator buzzes again and the doors open. You expected to find yourself on the helipad, but instead you're at the top corner of the platform, near the control tower where the sniper was shooting at you earlier. The sniper is gone now. She must have fled when the rig

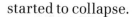

started to collapse.

Stacey leads you over to the edge. "We're going to jump," she says.

It's a long, long way down. Hitting the water from this distance would be like landing on concrete.

You stagger back from the edge, dizzy. "We can't!"

"We have to." Stacey backs away from the edge so she can take a running start. "Come on."

You don't move. "If we were going to jump, why didn't we do it on the other side? When it was only a thirty foot drop?"

"Kid," she says, "this rig will collapse any minute. There's no time to explain—just trust me."

Not trusting Stacey has gotten you into a lot of trouble today. But you're dead certain that a fall from this height will kill you.

The platform lurches. You wobble and almost pitch over into the ocean.

"We're out of time!" Stacey yells. She runs for the edge and reaches out to grab you.

If you take her hand, turn to page 26.
If you back away, turn to page 22.

0Y:03

You drag your feeble body across the dirt and dead grass until you reach the ditch. The thing that looked like a log isn't a log. It's your surfboard, already stained black with ash. This must be where the mercenaries first grabbed Agent Stacey, although the haze from the fire makes the forest look completely different.

You tumble into the ditch and pull your surfboard down on top of you. The fiberglass shell bumps your cheek. Broken rocks and twigs prod your back through your wetsuit.

You hope the dirt walls of the ditch will absorb the heat of the explosion, and the board will protect you from raining debris. But what if a great big tree lands on it? What if you get trapped, or buried alive? What if smoke inhalation kills you before the bomb even—

KABOOM!

The vibrations turn your insides to water. The flames instantly go out as all the oxygen is sucked into the explosion. You're suddenly dizzy. A thousand tons of dirt are catapulted into the air, turning the sky black.

You almost have time to scream before it all comes back down. The boiling mud pours out of the sky, slamming against your surfboard and filling the ditch around you, burning your skin. The roaring sound drowns out your hammering heart.

The black spots at the edge of your vision fade away as the oxygen returns to the air. You can see a crack of daylight between your board and the crush of mud around you. You're alive.

You try to push your board off so you can get out of the ditch, but it seems to weigh as much as a dead elephant. Either you've been weakened by your ordeal—entirely possible—or there's a whole heap of dirt and rubble on top of the board.

"Hrrrrrrrgh!" You push again with all your might. Useless. The board doesn't budge an inch . . .

But the wall of the ditch next to you shifts.

You start clawing at the hot mud. Maybe you can dig your way out.

Then the side of the ditch collapses completely, and you find yourself falling!

In a split second you realize what has happened. The explosion left a tremendous crater in the earth, and your ditch is right on the edge of it. Now the side of the ditch is collapsing into the crater, and you're about to fall in after it.

If you grab the nearest rock, turn to page 40.
If you grab the surfboard, turn to page 30.

The bad guys have a head start, but Stacey's boots have left trails in the forest floor. You follow them into the trees, treading carefully. You have no shoes—now would be a bad time to step on a sharp stick.

The trail dead-ends at a cluster of bushes. You look around.

There! A glimpse of the two mercenaries between the trees in the far distance. They're still dragging Agent Stacey. Her arms and legs are floppy. She's unconscious, or worse.

Once they're out of sight again, you keep moving.

Soon you come across a small campsite—not yours. A low tent, spray-painted green and brown to match the foliage, is pitched between two big trees. A satellite dish stands in a clearing nearby, pointing at the sky. A big metal box is padlocked shut beside a pile of camouflage netting. But where is Agent Stacey?

"*Mmmf!*"

There she is, under the netting. You can only see her wide eyes and the duct tape over her mouth. But at least she's alive.

She looks right at you. "*Mmmmf!*"

You're about to run across the clearing to help her

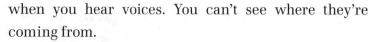

when you hear voices. You can't see where they're coming from.

"What's the problem?" one of the giants is asking.

"Something broke the laser trip wire," the other says.

"Could be an animal."

"Or maybe that kid followed us. I'll check it out."

You can't see the two guys yet. Maybe you have time to run over, free Stacey, and escape together before they arrive.

Then again, maybe you don't. You could dart into the bushes surrounding the clearing instead.

If you run to Stacey, turn to page 121.

If you hide in the bushes, turn to page 57.

You slam your hand down on the keyboard, hitting every button at once.

"No!" the boss yells.

The countdown stops.

You run for the door. Maybe you can still save Agent Stacey—

But once again, it looks like she doesn't need saving. You watch through the window in amazement as she wriggles out of the security guard's grip and stands up, banging her head on the underside of his chin. He topples like a building in a controlled demolition.

The boss reaches for something in his pocket, but Stacey crash-tackles him before he can get to it. He hits the ground, wheezing and Stacey holds him down.

"Daniel Winston Christie," she says, taking a pair of handcuffs out of her backpack. "You're under arrest. You have the right to remain silent."

"You'll never get off this rig," Christie spits.

Stacey raises an eyebrow. "Won't I?"

You can hear the drone of a helicopter approaching. A voice echoes through a megaphone. "This is the police. Vacate the landing pad immediately."

"Sounds like our ride is here," Stacey says, hauling Christie to his feet.

It doesn't seem real. Less than half an hour ago you were standing on the beach, contemplating a surf. Now you're on an offshore mining platform with a federal agent and a corrupt mining official. You've just prevented an enormous explosion from killing your friends and destroying a national park.

"If I tell anyone about this . . ." you begin.

"You'll end up in detention," Stacey reminds you. "This is all highly classified."

She must be able to see how disappointed you are. She puts a hand on your shoulder.

"But you did well, kid," she says. "Really well. Let's go take a ride in a helicopter."

00:00

You survived! There are twelve other ways to escape the danger—try to find them all!

As the helicopter thunders closer, you run across a clearing to a tree trunk that has half fallen into a shallow ditch. Vines shroud the trunk—it's been there a long time. You should be able to conceal yourself beneath the vegetation.

You scramble over the trunk and tumble into the ditch. The sky is mostly concealed. But what if the helicopter has some kind of thermal camera on board?

You don't get time to finish this thought.

Boom!

The bomb explodes with the fury of a thousand suns. You scream as the ditch rocks around you like a canoe in a cyclone. The world flashes bright white and then fades to an ominous gray as a wave of smoke rolls over the top of you.

The tree trunk moans. Vines creak and snap.

"No!" You try to climb out of the ditch, but you're too slow. The trunk rolls inward like a dying brontosaurus, ready to squash you—

Crunch!

THE END.

Return to page 120 to try again!

"OK," you mutter. "Here goes nothing."

You grab the wires, already second-guessing yourself. Are you about to make a horrible mistake?

But you have to do this. Bravery, someone once told you, is doing the right thing even when you're scared.

You take a deep breath—

And wrench the wires out of the lump of T4.

Nothing happens.

After a moment, the timer fades to black.

A wild grin spreads across your face. You just disarmed a bomb! Prevented a crime! Saved lives, including your own!

Beep.

The sound didn't come from the timer. You look around.

Another flashing light. Another timer. Another bomb, sitting in the shadows. Ready to turn you to dust.

You should have guessed that just one charge wouldn't be enough to create the stadium-size explosion Stacey described. You look around for more bombs, but can't see any.

This timer is counting down more quickly. Each

second disappears in half a second. When you deactivated the first bomb, some kind of signal must have been sent to the other.

No problem, you tell yourself. You'll just disarm it the same way.

But the first bomb wasn't counting down so fast, and it wasn't beeping like that. What if the signal has activated some kind of alarm?

You tell yourself you don't have a choice. There's no time for you to get out of the blast radius . . .

But maybe you can carry the bomb to a place where it won't hurt anybody else.

If you try to disarm the second bomb, turn to page 104.
If you take the bomb out of the cave and look for somewhere to dump it, turn to page 131.

ERROR TIME UNKNOWN

"**W**here are we?" Pigeon demands. "When are we?"

You back away from the shuffling horde of zombies. "I don't know!" you cry. "What do we do?"

The nearest zombie groans, its gray lips tugging upward to reveal sallow teeth and a black, crumbling tongue. It reaches out for Pigeon. She kicks it in the chest. It stumbles backward, but more are right behind it.

"Take us somewhere else!" she yells.

"I don't know how!"

"Use the book!"

You look down at the book in your hands. Does it really have the power to get you out of this?

A circle of rotting arms closes in to claim you.

"Pick a new page!" Pigeon screams. "Quickly!"

Go back to your original adventure.

Harrison looks alarmed. "The camp is empty," he says. "We should get to a safe distance and contact the authorities."

You're relieved that he's believed you so quickly. "I don't have my phone."

"I've got an emergency radio in the car. This way."

"What about everyone else?"

"They're up at the lookout, watching the sunset," Harrison says. "Plenty of distance between them and the campsite—but we need to contact the police right away. Come on."

He must have taken your warning about the bomb seriously. You follow him up a narrow trail. In this direction, the cliffs block out the disappearing sun. Darkness shrouds the forest floor. It's hard to avoid stepping on sharp rocks.

Harrison has shoes, and he keeps getting ahead of you—you're struggling to keep up.

A distant keening splits the air.

"What was that?" you ask.

Harrison doesn't stop. "What was what?"

There it is again. It's like the wailing of a hungry baby.

"You don't hear that?" you ask.

Harrison pauses reluctantly. He listens to the distant scream.

"Just feral cats fighting," he concludes. "Nothing to worry about. Come on."

The screeching gets louder, and then suddenly stops. You wonder if that means one of the cats won the fight.

A shallow river gurgles up ahead. A row of stepping stones crosses the water. Fine sand spirals in the water between them like smoke.

And something else. As you follow Harrison onto the stepping stones, you peer down at the red stain creeping through the current.

"Harrison," you say. "There's blood in the water."

He looks down, and frowns. "No," he says. "That must be something else."

The screaming sound had come from upstream, before it was cut off so abruptly. Now a flow of blood is coming from that direction. What happened?

Obviously an animal has been killed. But by what?

And then you see it. A dark shape beneath the water, getting closer and closer. Soon you can make out a giant tail, curving left and right like a dancer's hips as massive claws paddle beneath it.

An ancient fear surfaces in your brain. There's something more scary than a bomb in this forest. Something that can swim and think. Something with teeth.

"Crocodile!" you scream.

Harrison spins around—too quickly. He loses his balance on a stepping stone. Arms spinning, eyes wide with terror, he splashes down into the water.

The crocodile immediately changes direction. It swims toward Harrison, rows of fangs glimmering on either side of its enormous snout.

If you run over to Harrison and try to pull him out of the water, turn to page 54.

If you try to distract the crocodile, turn to page 7.

09:21

"OK," you say. "I'm sorry. I don't know what I was thinking."

"No offence taken," Harrison says. It's true—he doesn't look offended. That's what makes you sure you were right. If someone had accused you of being a dangerous criminal, you wouldn't have let it go so easily.

Harrison puts the phone back in his pocket. "Ready to head to the lookout? Everyone's waiting."

"Well . . ." you say, but he's already walking away toward the forest. You run to catch up.

A dirt bike lies on its side near the mouth of a narrow trail. Harrison picks up a pink helmet and tosses it to you. "We're running too late to walk now," he says, picking up another helmet for himself. "We'd better take this."

Late for what? you wonder. Meeting the others at the lookout, or getting out of range of the bomb?

Harrison straddles the dirt bike and guns the engine. You climb on behind him and wrap your arms around his waist.

He doesn't wait for you to get settled. He twists the throttle and launches the bike up the trail at a reckless pace. The dirt is so rough that your legs barely touch the seat as the bike bounces up the mountain.

You still don't trust him, but suddenly you realize he might not trust you either. He might realize you still suspect him. If that's the case, he might be taking you to somewhere other than the lookout.

But he's going too fast for you to jump off. Branches whip past, cracking against your helmet and the sleeves of your wetsuit. Harrison gets it worse, but he doesn't slow down.

"Be careful!" you shout, but there's no way he'll hear you over the roaring of the engine.

You shoot past a deep gully and around a tight bend before the lookout comes into view. Harrison wasn't lying—at least not about your destination. Pigeon, Neil, Shelley, and the other three kids lean against the wooden rail, staring out at the sunset.

Now's your chance to warn them. About the bomb, and Harrison.

"Watch out!" you yell to the distant group. "Harrison is—"

Boom!

You're a long way from the bomb when it goes off, but the shockwave still pushes you off the bike. You hit the dirt as a wall of superheated air sweeps over you.

Your friends are all knocked down by the blast. The bike slides out from under Harrison. He hits the ground and rolls over and over. The bike shrieks as it hits a tree and folds in half, shooting metal splinters all over the clearing. Gasoline spills out of the cracked fuel tank.

You stand up, ears ringing. Distant parts of the forest are ablaze. Sparks rain down from the sky. It looks like the end of the world.

The others stumble toward you. They look like extras in a zombie film, their clothes ripped from when they fell and stained by the ash blowing on the wind.

"..." Shelley says.

You wiggle a finger in your ear. "What?"

". . . you all right?" Shelley asks again. Her voice seems to come from a long way away.

"I'm OK, I think," you say. "But look!"

The falling sparks have ignited the puddle of fuel under the smashed dirt bike. You're standing downwind of the flames—the fire is spreading through the trees toward the lookout, fast.

"This way!" Pigeon starts running for the nearest trail, but the flames get there first. A curtain of fire sweeps across the entrance and Pigeon stumbles back. You're surrounded.

"There's no way out!" she cries.

It's true. All the trails are blocked, and the fire is crackling and spitting louder and louder, closer and closer, as if it's trying to herd you off the cliff. Everyone backs up to the wooden rail. The heat bakes your dry skin.

You have an idea. You lean over the rail and look down. The cliffs aren't sheer. There might just be enough hand- and footholds to climb down to the ocean.

"We'll never make it," Neil says.

"We have to try," you say.

"What about Harrison?" Shelley demands.

You'd forgotten all about him. He's still sprawled on the dirt near the burning bike. The flames are creeping closer to his outstretched hand.

If you try to save him, both of you might be burned alive. And you're ninety percent sure he knew about the bomb. But can you really leave him to die?

Every second counts.

If you climb down the cliffs, turn to page 126.
If you try to save Harrison, turn to page 19.

You emerge from your shelter. The sight of the beach takes your breath away. Even through the coiling steam and the sizzling rain, you can see that the shore-line looks like a war zone. A great chunk of the beach is missing, and the ocean has flooded in to fill the gap.

Crack. Roots snap behind you and the oak tree comes crashing down. You just step out of the way in time, and it hits the dirt with an epic boom.

You look around. Nothing else seems to be plotting to kill you. No more bombs, giants, treacherous camp leaders, or homicidal trees. The rain makes you uncomfortable, but no more than a slightly-too-hot shower. You seem to be OK.

A glimmer catches your eye on the horizon. Atop the distant lookout a police car has parked, lights swirling. It looks like Agent Stacey managed to contact the authorities after all. You hope they're arresting Harrison.

But you'd better make sure. You sigh heavily and begin the long walk up the hill.

00:00

You survived! There are twelve other ways to escape the danger—try to find them all!

You spin around to face the big croc. It looks like a dinosaur—something from millions of years ago, designed to crush and kill.

The croc's eyes roll backward and its jaw pops open as it launches itself forward, wet claws churning up the dirt. You throw yourself sideways into the bushes.

The crocodile shoots past you like a freight train. As you crash down into the foliage, the croc slams into a nearby tree. It snorts and snuffles like an enraged bull.

It turns, sees you in the bushes, and charges again.

But now you know what to do. With its eyes rolled back like that—for protection, you guess—it can't see while it's running at you. You just have to find a place to hide.

You crawl out of the way as the croc hurtles past again, jaws snapping as it plunges through the bushes. You scramble to your feet and run deeper into the forest, looking for a hiding place.

But the croc is learning just as fast as you are. It has already turned around and is running after you. And it knows this forest better than you do—as you run up a slight slope, the croc goes in a slightly different direction. Soon you realize why. The trail dead ends here.

The croc is blocking the only escape route.

You can't outsmart this thing. It has a lifetime of experience hunting down squishier animals. This time, when it charges, its eyes don't roll back.

You try to dive out of the way as the crocodile lunges at you, jaws first—

Boom!

The explosion illuminates the forest like a lightning bolt. A hot flash of energy zips outward from the horizon, frying leaves and blackening rocks. The airborne crocodile is between you and the distant bomb, but even shielded by its leathery weight, the blast still knocks you off your feet.

You hit the ground and roll out of the way just in time. The croc slams down to the forest floor, its charred hide smoking. It hisses, blinded by the light.

You lie still, too stunned to move. If the croc attacks you, you're done for.

But it doesn't. It bares some yellow teeth, hisses again, and stumbles away into the trees, one leg dragging behind it.

Without the crocodile, the bomb would have fried you. And without the bomb, the crocodile would have eaten you. It's almost too much to process.

You climb to your feet. The trees have reverse shadows—pale outlines beneath them where they blocked the flying ash. You walk across the dirty ground, your feet slowly becoming black. It's time to find Harrison and the others.

You wonder what happened to Agent Stacey . . .

00:00

You survived! There are twelve other ways to escape the danger—try to find them all!

03:55

A nearby tree has many stiff branches, each about as thick as a baseball bat. Plenty of handholds. You run to the tree, leap up to the lowest branch, and haul yourself out of the croc's reach.

It can outswim you, and maybe outrun you, but you're betting it can't outclimb you. Humans are primates. You come from a long line of climbers. You share DNA with monkeys and apes. You must be safe up here.

The crocodile reaches the bottom of the tree and stops dead. It looks up at you with evil, hungry eyes.

It circles around the tree once, twice. Your heart sinks. You had hoped the croc would give up and go away. There's no sign of Harrison. How long will you have to wait? If it doesn't leave, how will you get down?

The croc has its own ideas about that.

It rears up like a startled horse and grips the tree trunk with its forepaws. You gasp. No. Surely it can't climb up here?

But it doesn't need to. It shakes the tree vigorously, using all its weight—a ton of strong lizard muscle. Twigs scratch your face. A knot of wood painfully pinches your shoulder. You cling desperately to the branches like a frightened koala, but it's almost impossible to hang on.

"Help!" you scream. "Somebody! Help!"

But it's too late. The branches slip out of your grip and you fall, breaking sticks and bouncing off boughs as you fall toward the crocodile's waiting mouth . . .

Snap!

THE END.

Go back to page 83 to try again!

28:43

"**OK,** Leah," the woman says. "I'm Federal Agent Stacey. I would show you my ID, but I've left it in my other pants."

You laugh, but she doesn't appear to be kidding.

"Everyone at that camp is in danger," she repeats. "My GPS is busted—I can't get there by myself. I need you to show me the way right now."

"What's going on?"

She spits on the sand. "Listen, kid," she says. "Either you take me to the camp, or I'll arrest you for obstruction of justice."

The campsite isn't far away, but she hasn't shown you any proof that she's really an agent. She could be dangerous. Maybe you should lead her up the hill to the lookout. There are always lots of tourists up there around sunset—she won't try anything with so many people around.

Do you lead her to the camp, or the lookout? Make your choice and turn to page 10.

05:50

"**S**he didn't tell me much," you say. "No names. I didn't even see any proof that she was a real government agent."

Shelley is staring at you as if you're a crazy person. You wonder if she thinks Stacey is an agent—or if she thinks you're making the whole thing up.

Hunt sounds satisfied. "OK. What about these kidnappers? Would you recognize them if you saw them again?"

Probably not. They disappeared with Stacey pretty quickly.

"Well," you say. "They were wearing—"

Boom!

The explosion hits you from behind, throwing you against the man whose phone you borrowed. A wall of heat and light sweeps over you and the other campers.

You can't see anything, but you can hear Pigeon screaming. The guy you smashed into is underneath you, not moving. Maybe he hit his head when he fell.

You stand on shaking legs, rubbing your eyes. You're still blinded by the light and the grit in the air. "Is everyone OK?" you shout.

"What was that?" Neil yells.

"I guess there really was a bomb," you say, blinking furiously. "Shelley? Pigeon? Are you all right?" Your vision returns in time for you to see that half the forest is still hanging in the air. The explosion has kicked trees and rocks and dirt up into the sky, and now they're starting to come back down.

Thump! A tremendous lump of dirt hits the ground next to you.

Crack! A lump of rock smashes the wooden handrail to splinters.

"Run!" you yell, but it's too late. The enormous bough of a gum tree plummets out of the sky, trailing smoke, headed right for you—

THE END.

For another try, return to page 110.

The silence is marred only by the grinding of crickets. You breathe through your nose, making the fallen leaves dance around your face.

Stacey releases your mouth. "Sorry," she says. "The mining company hired mercenaries to plant the explosives. They might still be—"

Two men charge out of the bushes. Both are huge, with massive shoulders and thick necks. Their camouflage uniforms made them invisible until they moved.

You scramble back across the dirt. Stacey reaches behind her for some kind of weapon, but she's too slow. The two giants grab her wrists before she can get to it.

"I'm a federal agent," she yells. "You're breaking the law!"

Neither of the giants respond. They drag Stacey into the trees and disappear, leaving you alone on the path. They must not consider you important—maybe they think you'll be blown up at sunset.

You stand up shakily. Suddenly this has all become very real, and you believe everything Stacey has told you.

If you follow the two giants, you might be able to save Stacey somehow. Then she can find and disarm the bomb. But those guys seem ruthless and highly trained.

Maybe you'd be better off running to the camp and warning everyone about the bomb instead.

If you chase after Stacey and her abductors, turn to page 75.

If you head for the camp, turn to page 117.

You crouch down beside the explosive like a vet next to a sick but dangerous animal. You have no cutting tools. It won't be like in the movies, where the hero snips one of the wires, and somehow gets it right. You're going to have to just rip the wires out and hope for the best.

Fortunately, there only seem to be two real options. You can either pull the wires out of the timer, or out of the lump of explosive.

Your trembling hands hover over the bomb.

If you rip the wires out of the timer, turn to page 104.

If you pull them out of the lump of T4, turn to page 80.

You duck behind the rock and scan the horizon. Still no one in sight. The forest is dark and quiet. Insects buzz in the foliage, and the trees sway like zombies.

You wait. The bomb doesn't go off. Perhaps it was a dud. It feels like enough time must have passed for the counter to reach zero.

You clench your teeth so hard that they hurt. Maybe you did have time to reach a safe distance. Maybe you still do.

You decide to stay put. After all, what if—

BOOM!

The explosion rips through the forest like a tornado, tearing up the dirt and flinging trees like matchsticks. The sound pierces your eardrums. You can't even hear yourself screaming. The sky goes black with dust.

By the time you realize the big rock is shifting, it's too late. Your foot is already caught under its crushing weight.

Fortunately you're not in pain for very long. The rock rolls right over you, and then the whole world disappears.

THE END.

Go back to page 32 to try again!

You flop on the dry sand and start digging like a crazy dog. For every two handfuls of sand you pull out, one handful slides back in. But you dig with such desperation you're soon hunched over a very shallow ditch.

You're still digging when the bomb goes off.

At first the explosion is silent—just a sudden flare of blinding light. Then the wall of energy hits you like a train, shoving you into the ditch. The world turns upside down, the ocean replacing the sky.

The noise reaches you then. It's the sound of a swimming pool's worth of water suddenly becoming steam. But you don't hear it for long, because an avalanche of wet sand thunders down on top of you, plugging your ears and pressing your face into the ground.

Silence.

Too late, you realize that you can't move. The mountain of sand is crushing your chest, squeezing the air out of your lungs. When you thought you were making shelter, you were actually digging your own grave.

You scream, and sand fills up your mouth.

THE END.

Go back to page 80 to try again!

07:01

You exhale shakily. You wrap your fingers around the wire. It's warm, even through the plastic insulation. Current is definitely running through the copper within.

You wonder if this will be your last act. You wonder if anyone will ever know what happened to you.

"One," you whisper. "Two. Three!"

You yank the wires out.

There's a brilliant flash—

THE END.

Go back to page 32 to try again!

01:01

You sail over the dark gap, feet kicking the air, an involuntary battle cry escaping your throat.

But the gap is still getting wider. The heavy earth shifts, cracking and moaning. The chasm looks hundreds of feet deep, lined with rocks as sharp as knives. You're not going to make it . . .

But you do! You hit the ground on the other side and slip over immediately, landing on your back in the hot dust.

"You OK?" Shelley calls.

But it's suddenly too loud to reply. With a sound like rolling thunder, the cliff collapses behind you. You turn your head in time to see the lookout fall away, smashing down into the black ocean below.

00:00

You survived! There are twelve other ways to escape the danger—try to find them all!

You lean overboard and paddle with your hands. The hovercraft drifts slowly behind one of the concrete pylons. Now if anyone opens the hatch, they won't be able to see you. They would have to climb down the harpoon cable to get to you.

You sit on the floor of the hovercraft, suddenly exhausted, wondering what's happening on dry land. Have the cops managed to evacuate the camp? Will they know where you are? Stacey didn't tell them over the phone that you were with her. You hope no one goes back to look for you. When the bomb goes off, will you hear it from this distance?

The motor whirs, keeping the hovercraft floating on a cushion of air. The only other sound is the choppy water lapping against the rubber skirt . . .

And the hissing, which is suddenly louder.

You peer over the edge. The syringe which was stuck into the rubber is now gone. The air pressure beneath must have popped it out, leaving a tear about the size of a pea. Now the skirt is deflating.

The hovercraft tilts to one side. Water spills over the edge onto the floor. You look around for something to bail with, but there are no buckets.

You cup your hands in the water and throw it overboard, but it's like trying to serve rice with tweezers. The hovercraft sinks deeper and deeper—

Then the motor gets waterlogged and dies.

Without the air pressure holding it up, the craft drops like a stone. It disappears under the water and sinks into the gray ocean, leaving you treading water alone between the pylons. The harpoon gun dangles in the air, out of reach.

Your teeth chatter. It's getting dark, and the water is very cold this far away from the beach.

Now what? You could swim to shore—you're a good swimmer, so it would probably only take six or seven minutes. But someone might shoot you with a tranquilizer dart on the way, and you'd drown. Even if you made it to the beach, you might get blown up if the cops don't get to the bomb in time.

You can't stay here. Eventually the bad guys will come looking for you, or you'll get too tired to swim, and . . .

Something bubbles to the surface. It's one of the big fans, floating on its own. A few more bits of the hovercraft bob up—part of the skirt and a chunk of the hull. It must have gotten smashed somehow.

A shadow sweeps past under the water. At first you think more pieces of the hovercraft are coming back up. But no—this is something much bigger.

Whatever it is, the shadow doesn't stay long. It

descends back to the depths.

Several questions rush through your mind at once. Why wasn't it "safe" for the company to drill in the ocean anymore? Why do these people have tranquilizer rifles? And was that really just a patch of seaweed you saw under the water, before Stacey's boat limped into shore?

You swim over to the nearest concrete pylon and cling to it, but other than the barnacles, it's smooth. You can't climb out of the water.

The shadow reappears, directly beneath you. Details form in the darkness as the shape races for the surface.

Fins. Eyes. Teeth!

You scrabble at the pylon, dragging yourself around to the other side of it, away from the rising predator. The creature bursts forth from the ocean, gnashing its tremendous fangs.

You scream. It's a shark, but not just any shark. It's huge, with a nose as big as the hood of a car and eyes the size of soccer balls. Another fin breaks the surface about sixty feet away, and it takes you a minute to realize that it's the tail fin of this same creature.

This must be a new species of giant shark. Or maybe a really old, undiscovered one.

The monster chomps on the pylon. It misses you, but comes so close that you feel the rush of air as its jaws sweep past. It sinks back into the depths and disappears, leaving a couple of teeth the size of shovel heads wedged into the concrete.

You stare down into the black ocean, heart racing. You remember reading somewhere that a shark can detect a human pulse from miles away. This thought doesn't make your heart beat any slower.

Stacey's rope still dangles from the harpoon above, but now that the hovercraft has sunk, it's out of reach by several feet. You can't escape that way.

"Help!" you scream. Maybe someone from the platform above will come to your rescue. But the rig above is still and silent.

At any moment the shark will return to bite you in half with those gigantic teeth. No one will ever know what happened to you.

You could swim for the shore. The shark is so big that it probably can't come into shallow water. But the shore is almost half a mile away, and you can't possibly swim as fast as the shark can.

Maybe you should try to climb onto the floating fan instead. Get out of the water and wait for help.

If you swim for the beach, turn to page 123.
If you climb up on the fan, turn to page 41.

"What?" you ask.

Stacey examines the surrounding trees like a wild animal watching for predators.

Leaves rustle. Boughs creak.

"What?" you say again.

"The mercenaries hired to plant the explosives might still be here," Stacey whispers. "Keep your voice—"

She doesn't get any farther before she is slammed off her feet. A big man swinging on a rope has crashed into her at high speed, and now they're both soaring away into the jungle like Tarzan and Jane.

You stumble backward, dropping your board, so shocked, you almost fall over too. Through the trees, you see the man let go of the rope. He and Stacey drop to the ground, where another man in camouflage gear grabs Stacey's wrists so she can't struggle. The two men drag her into the forest and disappear.

You stare after them, flabbergasted. It all happened so fast. What should you do?

This sudden abduction leads you to believe that Agent Stacey was telling the truth: the bomb is real. With no hope of finding or defusing it yourself, maybe you should continue up to the lookout. There's bound to be someone with a phone up there. You could call 911 so they send police to evacuate everyone from the blast zone.

But there might not be time to get everybody out. What if Stacey is the only one who knows where the bomb is and how to defuse it? Maybe you should chase after the two mercenaries and try to help her escape.

If you chase after the men and try to rescue Stacey, turn to page 75.
If you run up to the lookout to summon help, turn to page 47.

03:03

You wrap your hands around the nearest bough just in time. A wall of hot air slams into you, lifting your feet off the ground.

It's like being caught in a hurricane on the surface of the sun. The fire sucks the air out of your lungs, scorching your skin and melting your wetsuit.

Just as suddenly, it's over. The flames vanish, the roaring stops, and you flop to the ground like a discarded puppet. The ringing in your ears is disorienting. You wonder if you still have eyebrows.

But you're not dead. Even though it seems impossible, you survived the explosion.

From where you're lying, you can see the lights flash at the top of the hill. Blue and red—the cops have reached the lookout. You guess Agent Stacey must have escaped and gotten the word out. You hope her colleagues are arresting the bombers right now.

You climb up and wait for the world to stop spinning. Then you begin the long hike to the lookout.

00:00

You survived! There are twelve other ways to escape the danger— try to find them all!

Harrison chuckles nervously. "OK, you got me. Very funny."

"I'm serious!" you insist. "You need to call the police so they can tell us how to defuse the bomb. And everyone needs to help with the search. It's somewhere in the caves near here."

You look around. No one is sitting around the fire, and you can't hear anybody talking in the tents. "Hey, where is everyone?" you ask.

"At the lookout," Harrison says. "Stargazing."

This seems silly, since it's not yet dark enough for the stars to be out. But you're pretty sure the lookout will be outside the blast radius, so your friends are probably safe.

Unfortunately, that means they can't help you search for the bomb.

"So," Harrison says. "Can we drop all this nonsense and go join them?"

You expected him to take the threat more seriously. "I'm telling the truth!" you say. "A federal agent warned me that there was a—"

"A federal agent?" Harrison asks, looking suddenly alarmed. "When was this?"

"Just a couple of minutes ago. At the beach."

"And what did she tell you exactly?"

"She said—"

You stop talking. Because you don't remember telling Harrison the agent was female. Did he just guess?

And why did he schedule a stargazing expedition so far away from camp, at a time when it's not even dark enough to see any stars?

"What did she say?" Harrison demands.

Is he taking your story more seriously because the federal authorities are involved? Or does he know something about the bomb, and he's worried about getting found out?

If you accuse Harrison of knowing about the bomb, turn to page 50.
If you trust Harrison and tell him everything you know about Agent Stacey, turn to page 39.

You bolt out of the cave and race back the way you came, desperate to get out of range. Soon you hit the point at which this trail splits off from the main path.

No sign of Harrison. There's so little time left that he's probably given up searching for you and is fleeing for his life.

You turn back toward the lookout and run. Prickles stick into the soles of your bare feet. Branches scratch your face, unleashing clouds of excited insects. It's getting harder to see in the fading light.

You keep running until you reach the big rock. You don't know how many seconds you have left. Maybe you should take cover and wait for the blast.

Then again, you're not that far from the cave— certainly not a stadium-length away. The explosion might still cook you at this distance. Perhaps you should keep running.

If you take cover behind the big rock, turn to page 102.
If you keep running, turn to page 9.

You strike out for the shoreline, leaving the stunned shark behind. The water hisses and bubbles, still hot from the explosion. It's hard to swim through the foam, but anything is better than facing those gigantic teeth.

Suddenly you can hear voices. Someone is screaming your name.

You blink saltwater out of your eyes and look around. The wrecked beach is deserted. Did you imagine it?

No. Someone at the lookout above is waving their arms wildly. It's hard to tell, but it looks like Neil, one of your friends from surf camp. He survived the explosion!

You can see Pigeon and Shelley behind him. And Harrison. Everyone's OK!

Now that Neil has your attention, he yells something.

"What?" you shout.

"Shark!" he screams.

The shark must have recovered from the blast. You swim even harder, but you're already exhausted. The water feels as thick as honey. You wonder how far behind you the shark—CHOMP!

THE END.

Go back to page 106 to try again!

You run as fast as you can to the camp, leaving your board behind. You can't believe how suddenly your day has turned into a nightmare. There are mercenaries in the jungle, and they've just kidnapped a federal agent in front of your eyes.

Your friends have no idea of the danger they're in. You need to get them out of the blast radius—or find and disarm the bomb.

Soon you see the towels fluttering on the clothesline and ashes in the fire pit beyond. This is the camp. But where are the people?

"Harrison?" you call.

Your voice echoes around the campsite. There's no answer.

"Pigeon?" you try. "Shelley? Neil?"

No one responds.

A plastic storage box lies at your feet, filled with emergency supplies. Maybe there's a phone inside—or at least a note explaining where everyone went.

You open the box. There's a coil of rope, a box of matches, and some cans of beans. No note, no phone.

You can't afford to waste any more time. You'll have to flee. But maybe you should take some of this gear with you. It could be useful for when you're escaping the blast zone—or if you see Agent Stacey and have an opportunity to help her.

Do you pick up the rope, or the matches? Make your choice, and turn to page 138.

01:01

You fly over the gap, legs kicking, arms flailing. Neil is on the other side, reaching out for you—

But the chasm is widening even as you cross it. Deadly blackness yawns below you, spiked with sharp rocks. The cliffs roar as they collapse, stone grinding on stone.

Your clutching hand misses Neil's.

"Noooooo!" you scream, as you plunge down into the darkness.

THE END.

Go back to page 47 to try again!

09:21

You reach out for the phone.

Just as you're about to grab it, Harrison pushes a button. Twin prongs sprout from the end of the phone. It's not a phone at all. It's some kind of—

He jabs the device against your upper arm. There's a crackling sound and your teeth slam together against your will, as though you're a ventriloquist's dummy. Your arms and legs lock together and you topple over.

Harrison catches you just before you hit the ground.

"Shhhhhhh," he says.

You black out.

When you wake up all your muscles are sore. You're lying in the dirt. Harrison is gone, clearly happy to abandon you here. He must not think you have enough time to escape from the blast and expose his treachery.

Time to prove him wrong. But how?

Your gaze settles on the row of tents and the still-smoldering campfire. You might be able to science up an experimental escape vehicle. Perhaps you can heat the air inside one of the tents and float away.

Or maybe that's insane. Perhaps you should just run.

If you sprint away as fast as you can, turn to page 3.

If you try to turn one of the tents into a hot air balloon, turn to page 27.

You race across the clearing, rip off the camouflage netting, and reach for the tape across Stacey's lips—

But she grabs your hands and stops you.

She's not tied up. Duct tape is around her wrists, but it's torn. She's free. She was only pretending to be bound.

You're still processing this—and realizing that "*Mmmf!*" meant "Go away, you're about to ruin everything"—when she drags you to the ground and pulls the camouflage netting over both of you.

Just in time. The two mercenaries walk into view.

"Did you hear something?" one asks.

"Yeah." The other mercenary gestures to the netting. "She must be awake."

"I'll get the tranquilizer." The first giant goes over to the metal box and hesitates. "Hey. Did you lock this?"

"No. I left it open for you."

"Then why is it—"

Stacey doesn't wait any longer. She leaps up and throws the netting over one of the mercenaries. He whirls around and gets hopelessly tangled in a matter of seconds. He yells, panicked.

The other guy hurls a huge fist at Stacey, but he's too slow. She ducks under his arm, reaches up, and sprays something on his face from an aerosol can.

He blinks, sniffs, and falls over like an uprooted tree.

The first guy has managed to fight his way out of the net, but not quickly enough to get away from Agent Stacey. She sprays the same thing on his face. He hits the dirt like a dead rhinoceros.

"Wow," you say.

"Get up," Stacey orders. "We have to move."

"Where are we going?"

Ignoring you, she digs through the pockets of one of the fallen mercenaries until she finds a phone.

"Come on," she says. "We have to get back to the oil rig."

One word stands out in that sentence. "'We'?"

Stacey picks up her backpack and puts it on. "Right. I can't operate the hovercraft by myself."

"Hovercraft?!"

Go to page 133.

You push off the pylon and swim freestyle to the beach. Your stroke is long and powerful, but you wince at every splash. Surely the shark can hear you flailing desperately against the water.

Then again, maybe it's given up. It might have lost so many teeth biting that concrete that it's decided to go home to wherever it is that giant sharks live. Or maybe it spotted bigger prey and decided to eat that instead.

It is hard to resist the urge to peer down into the dark water, looking for signs of the shark beneath you.

It's like walking a tightrope. Focus on going in a straight line, you tell yourself. Don't look down.

You can't work out how far you've traveled. The oil platform is a long way behind you, but the shore doesn't look any closer. The surf gets rougher as you swim through shallower waters.

Suddenly the water seems thicker. The current is turning against you, pulling you back toward the oil rig. A big wave must be building behind you. Maybe you can ride it all the way to shore.

You turn to look at the wave, trying to judge where it will break—

And then you see something through the curtain of

shimmering water. A giant ring of teeth.

The shark is inside the wave, rushing right for you, with its mouth open.

You paddle desperately, trying to get out of the way. The wave looms taller and taller, foaming at the top as it gets closer. You can see the shark's emotionless eyes behind the murky water, zooming in on you. A scarred fin breaks through the surface.

You cover your head with your arms as the wave crashes down on top of you—

THE END.

Return to page 133 to try again!

The box of matches is still tucked under the sleeve of your wetsuit. You rip it out, shake a match loose, and strike it, hoping that they didn't get wet when you jumped into the waist-deep water.

They didn't. The match fizzes as a bright flame flares to life. You hold it in front of you like an Olympic baton.

The croc slows down. It's impossible to tell what's happening inside its ruthless reptilian brain. Perhaps it's afraid of the fire. Or maybe it's just confused because its prey isn't trying to escape.

Either way, you're not safe for long. The croc has you cornered, and the bomb could go off at any minute.

The crocodile creeps forward, claws unfurling.

The match flickers and dies.

You strike another one. *Hiss.* But the croc doesn't back off. Its tail swooshes from side to side.

You flick the match straight into the crocodile's eye.

Direct hit! But your elation evaporates when the croc doesn't flinch. The croc's jaws pop open and it leaps at you—

Crunch!

THE END.
Go back to page 83 to try again!

03:04

"**L**eave him," you shout, and climb over the rail.

"What?!" Pigeon yells.

"There's no time." You start climbing down the cliffs. The rocks are slippery, worn away by millennia of ocean gales. Neil climbs over the rail after you.

"I'm going back for Harrison!" Pigeon sprints back down toward the fire.

"No!" you yell. "He knew about the bomb! He risked all of our lives!"

But Pigeon keeps running toward Harrison.

"What are you talking about?" Neil demands.

"Pigeon!" you scream. But it's too late. The fire swarms in, trapping Pigeon. She vanishes into the glare.

The flames lick closer to the railing. Soon you'll be roasted.

"Climb down!" you shout.

You, Shelley, and Neil all scramble down the cliffs. It's hard to spot the handholds in the dying light. The wooden railing is already smoldering.

At one point you reach down for a foothold that isn't there.

"Argh!" You slip, and fall . . .

But only a foot. You catch an outcrop of stone in one hand and dangle there like a flag on a still day.

"You OK?" Neil yells.

You grab the outcrop with your other hand and haul yourself up. "We need to find another way down."

A rumbling sound is building. At first you think it's the fire, but then you realize it's something worse.

You turn to see that the ocean has receded—and now it's coming back. A massive wave is growing on the horizon, hurtling faster and faster toward the shore.

The explosion has triggered a tsunami. A million gallons of water are about to smash the three of you against the cliffs.

"Go back up!" you scream. "Quick!"

The others scramble back up the rock face. But going up is harder than going down. You're falling behind.

You risk a glance over your shoulder and realize that the wave is almost upon you.

"Noooo!" you scream, as the black water rises up to claim you—

Your head hits the stone and the world vanishes.

THE END.

Go back to page 50 to try again!

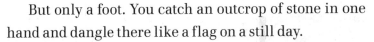

03:51

Wondering if you're totally crazy, you tie a loose knot in the rope and run toward the rampaging crocodile.

The monster slows down, confused. Before it has time to wonder why its prey isn't fleeing in terror, you wrap the loop of rope around its snout and cinch the knot tight.

The crocodile hisses, sounding like a flat truck tire as it fights to break the restraints. But it can't. The rope is strong, and the croc is surprisingly weak. The muscles that shut the croc's jaws must be much more powerful than the muscles that open them. As long as this rope is wrapped around the creature's giant head, it can't bite you.

The croc swipes at you with a giant paw. You barely get out of the way in time—the claws leave deep gouges in your wetsuit. Rather than chasing you, the crocodile shakes its head vigorously, trying to dislodge the rope.

"Quick!" Harrison yells. "Jump!"

While the croc is distracted, you sprint for the ditch. It's too deep for the crocodile to easily crawl across. But is it also too wide for you to leap over?

Hiss. The crocodile is chasing you again. It has fought

its way out of the loop. You run as fast as you can and hurl yourself across the small ravine—

But it's too wide, you're not going to make it—

And then Harrison grabs your outstretched hand and hauls you up on the other side.

You both collapse to the ground, breathing heavily. The croc prowls back and forth on the other side of the ditch, looking for a way across. Bits of rope hang from its teeth.

"Let's go," Harrison yells. You run up the hill together, out of the big croc's sight.

"How did you know that would work?" Harrison asks, panting.

"I didn't," you say.

Boom!

The explosion knocks you both down. It's like someone hit a timpani with a sledgehammer right behind your head. The sky goes black with flying debris. Only the thick canopy of leaves above stops you from being buried under a cloud of dust.

You'd forgotten all about the bomb. Lucky you traveled so far from the campsite, or you and Harrison might have been vaporized. Fortunately, the lookout is even farther away—your friends should be OK.

"Thanks," you say. "You saved my life."

Harrison looks oddly guilty. "You saved mine," he says. "Now come on. Let's get to the car."

As you trudge through the mess of pebbles and ash that now cover the forest floor, you wonder if your parents will ever let you go camping again.

00:00

You survived! There are twelve other ways to escape the danger—try to find them all!

05:49

Heart pounding, you scoop up the bomb—it's surprisingly light for something so powerful—and sprint out of the cave. The seconds blink away on the timer.

01:50, 01:49, 01:48 . . .

No sign of Harrison in the forest. You must have guessed correctly—he knew about the bomb, and now he's as far away from the blast radius as he can get. At the lookout with the other kids, probably.

With half as much explosive, you guess the explosion will be only half as big. But half the size of a stadium is still huge. You need to find a wide, flat area with no trees or rocks to get picked up and thrown about.

Suddenly you know the perfect place. But will you make it in time?

You sprint back along the trail, away from the camp. You pass the place where you left Harrison and take a fork to the left, racing past the spot where Stacey was attacked by the two giant goons. You keep glancing down at the timer and almost trip over your fallen surfboard.

00:59, 00:58 . . .

Finally you're at the beach. There's still no one around. You dash down the sand to the black ocean. Your feet kick up salty spray as you reach the shallows and keep going until you're waist deep in the cold waves. Then you hurl the bomb as far as you can.

Maybe the water will destroy the electronics and stop the explosive charge from detonating. Or maybe it will set the bomb off early. You don't wait around to find out. Before the bomb even hits the water you're already running in the opposite direction back to the shore.

Your feet drag in the undertow. It's like one of those nightmares where a monster is behind you and your legs won't move fast enough to outrun it.

Soon you hit the shore. You could run back up to the trees, but if the bomb goes off before you get there, you'll be fried. Maybe you should dig a trench for cover instead.

If you dig a hole in the sand to protect yourself from the blast, turn to page 103.

If you keep running to the tree line, turn to page 56.

11:03

tacey's already running into the trees, back toward the beach. You chase after her. Even with her limp, it's hard to keep up.

"What about the bomb?" you say. "What about my friends?"

"I can't make it to the caves in time to defuse the bomb," she says. "How close are the police helicopters?"

You look up. "I have no idea."

"OK," Stacey says, and you realize she's talking on the stolen phone. "I need one team to evacuate the campers, the other to defuse the bomb. I'm headed back to the oil rig to grab the ringleader."

She hangs up without saying goodbye.

"I don't know how to pilot a hovercraft," you say, puffing.

"It's fairly straightforward," she says. "And I can't leave you here. If they don't defuse the bomb in time . . ."

She leaves the sentence hanging. There's a sinking feeling. You had thought this was all over—that the good guys had won.

"If you have a hovercraft," you ask, "why were you in a wrecked speedboat?"

"I don't have one. Those guys did." She jerks a thumb back over her shoulder.

You emerge onto the beach. Stacey runs over to the mountain of sand you saw earlier—the one you thought had once been a big sandcastle. She clears away some of the sand, revealing a plastic tarpaulin just beneath the surface.

"They left it here when they came over to plant the bombs," Stacey says. "The sand was supposed to hide it from thermal cameras and satellites. I just hope the keys are in it. Give me a hand, will you?"

You run over and grab the tarp.

"On three," Stacey says. "One, two, three!"

You both pull the tarpaulin. It slides off, revealing a two-person hovercraft. Sand cascades over your bare feet.

Stacey jumps in. "Come on!"

You hesitate. The craft doesn't look as futuristic as you expected. It looks like an oversize bumper car with two big fans bolted to the back, protected by metal grilles. A rubber skirt hangs around the edge.

"Hurry up." Stacey grabs the key in the ignition and twists. The fans roar to life. The rubber skirt inflates. You climb into the hovercraft just in time. It starts to slide down the beach like a puck on an air hockey table.

"Hold them steady!" Stacey gestures at the fans. "You're steering."

You grab the swiveling bar attached to the fans. The word TILLER is engraved on it. "What will you be doing?"

The hovercraft reaches the water and glides right over it, bouncing on the gentle swells. Stacey grabs a harpoon gun from the floor of the vessel and starts reeling in the cable. "Don't worry about me. The rig's that way." She points slightly to your right.

You yank the tiller sideways. The big fans swivel. The hovercraft cruises around in a slow orbit, engine whining.

When the hovercraft rolls out from between the cliffs that surround the beach, the oil platform comes into view on the horizon. It looks like an enormous tabl, hovering above the ocean on four fat legs. Brightly colored shipping containers surround a watchtower on top. A crusted pipe sticks straight down into the ocean, sucking up oil from beneath the seabed.

"What's the plan when we get there?" you ask.

"You're staying here. I'm going up there to arrest the people in charge before they get airlifted out. A police helicopter will arrive for backup in ten or fifteen minutes."

"Won't the bad guys see us coming?"

"They've already seen us coming," Stacey says.

Something splashes into the water next to the hover-craft. A split second later you hear the pop of a gunshot.

"They're shooting at us!" you cry.

"Yes. I suggest you keep your head down."

Stacey doesn't heed her own advice. She remains upright at the bow like a figurehead of a mermaid on a ship, the harpoon gun balanced on her shoulder.

You stay low, cowering behind the rim of the hull. The hovercraft has almost reached the looming rig.

Another splash. Something hits the rubber skirt. You peep over the side to look. A syringe is sticking out of the skirt, featherlike tailpiece quivering in the wind.

"They're using poison darts!" you say.

"Ballistic tranquilizer," Stacey corrects. "Enough to knock out a hippo. If one of those syringes hits you, you'll be dead before you feel the sting."

"Why do they have that?!"

The hovercraft drifts into the shadow of the platform. Stacey crosses the hull to shut down the fans, leaving the craft floating between the gigantic concrete pylons. She aims the harpoon gun straight up and pulls the trigger.

Pow! The spear explodes out of the barrel. The reel whirs like a rattlesnake as the cable unspools. The harpoon punctures the underside of the platform with a distant thunk.

"Stay here," Stacey says. She hooks the gun onto the tiller, grabs the cable, and starts climbing up to the platform. It's at least fifty feet, but she gets to the top in less than thirty seconds.

"When will you be back?" you hiss.

"Soon." She opens a hidden hatch and scrambles up out of sight. The hatch falls closed after her.

You look around at the choppy water. The people on the rig know the hovercraft is down here. What if they open the hatch and start shooting at you? Maybe you should climb up there, too.

If you climb up after Stacey, turn to page 63.

If you stay in the hovercraft, turn to page 106.

If you climb up after Stacey, turn to page 63.
If you stay in the hovercraft, turn to page 106.

1850

"**H**ey! Where have you been?"

You look up from the storage box. Harrison, the camp leader, storms toward you. He's a stout man with hairy arms and a sunglasses tan. This is his first camp—there was a different leader when you came last year.

"Mr. Michaels!" you shout. Harrison told everyone they could call him by his first name, but the adrenaline has made you forget.

He turns his faded blue eyes on you. "I've been looking everywhere for you!" he growls. "What were you thinking, just wandering off?"

You don't know why he's angry. It's only a couple of minutes' walk to the beach, and kids are constantly wandering there and back again. But you don't have time to get defensive.

"There's a bomb near the camp!" you say.

Harrison's eyes go wide. The color drains from his face. "What?"

"A government agent showed up looking for it. We have to . . ."

If you say ". . . find the bomb and disarm it!," turn to page 113.

If you say ". . . get everyone as far away as possible!," turn to page 83.

The world ends right behind you. There's a blinding flash of light and a mighty blast of energy slams into your back, lifting you off your feet and throwing you forward. You just have time to cover your face with your arms before you crash into the nearest tree.

Smash! You cry out as you hit the trunk with bone-shattering force. But there's no time to even feel the pain as a wall of fire and debris swarms in to consume you.

THE END.

Go back to page 13 to try again!

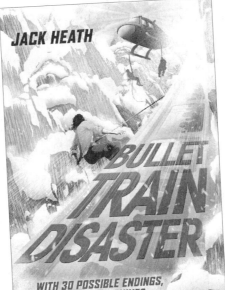